Blood Night

Also from Heather Graham

Blood Night
A Krewe of Hunters Novella
By Heather Graham

1001 Dark Nights

EVIL EYE
CONCEPTS

Blood Night
A Krewe of Hunters Novella
Copyright 2019 Heather Graham Pozzessere
ISBN: 978-1-970077-28-5

Foreword: Copyright 2014 M. J. Rose

Published by Evil Eye Concepts, Incorporated

This is a work of fiction. Names, places, characters and incidents are the product of the author's imagination and are fictitious. Any resemblance to actual persons, living or dead, events or establishments is solely coincidental.

Sign up for the 1001 Dark Nights Newsletter
and be entered to win a Tiffany Key necklace.

There's a contest every month!

Go to www.1001DarkNights.com to subscribe.

**As a bonus, all subscribers can download
FIVE FREE exclusive books!**

One Thousand and One Dark Nights

Once upon a time, in the future…

*I was a student fascinated with stories and learning.
I studied philosophy, poetry, history, the occult, and
the art and science of love and magic. I had a vast
library at my father's home and collected thousands
of volumes of fantastic tales.*

*I learned all about ancient races and bygone
times. About myths and legends and dreams of all
people through the millennium. And the more I read
the stronger my imagination grew until I discovered
that I was able to travel into the stories... to actually
become part of them.*

*I wish I could say that I listened to my teacher
and respected my gift, as I ought to have. If I had, I
would not be telling you this tale now.
But I was foolhardy and confused, showing off
with bravery.*

*One afternoon, curious about the myth of the
Arabian Nights, I traveled back to ancient Persia to
see for myself if it was true that every day Shahryar
(Persian: شهریار, "king") married a new virgin, and then
sent yesterday's wife to be beheaded. It was written
and I had read, that by the time he met Scheherazade,
the vizier's daughter, he'd killed one thousand
women.*

Something went wrong with my efforts. I arrived in the midst of the story and somehow exchanged places with Scheherazade – a phenomena that had never occurred before and that still to this day, I cannot explain.

Now I am trapped in that ancient past. I have taken on Scheherazade's life and the only way I can protect myself and stay alive is to do what she did to protect herself and stay alive.

Every night the King calls for me and listens as I spin tales. And when the evening ends and dawn breaks, I stop at a point that leaves him breathless and yearning for more. And so the King spares my life for one more day, so that he might hear the rest of my dark tale.

As soon as I finish a story... I begin a new one... like the one that you, dear reader, have before you now.

Prologue

Cheyenne Donegal could hear a slow but steady dripping sound as she sluggishly cracked open her eyes.

Her arms ached with a pain that nearly made her cry out, but something warned her to keep silent. A dull throb in her head pounded, and awareness and memory came to her at the same time.

She had been walking down Swain's Lane, the steep and unforgiving path that separated East Highgate Cemetery from West Highgate Cemetery.

She'd thought she had the answer to the killings…

And she had. But, sadly—oh so sadly—that seemed to be only part of it.

Her wrists were tied, and the middle of the rope binding them had been tossed over a hook suspended from the ceiling. The tension was the cause of the ache in her arms.

Her head pounded because of the smash from the *vampire's* cane that had cost her her consciousness.

And the drip?

Carefully opening her eyes wider, she looked around. It seemed to be an underground cavern or…no.

Not cavern.

Tomb.

The structure seemed to have been carved deep into the earth like other tombs, but it was slightly different. There were shelves, as in many mausoleums in Highgate. But not all of them held coffins.

Just…

Bodies. Corpses in various stages of decay. Stretched out on stone.

Cheyenne fought back a scream. She'd meant to keep her awareness of her situation a secret as long as possible until she discovered a way out, an escape, a means to find help.

But she was deep in the earth, she knew. And she doubted she was in either the east or the west section of the cemetery proper, but rather off to the side somewhere. In a tomb secretly dug years ago by someone known as the *vampire,* and now used to perhaps preserve the victims he held near and dear to his heart, instead of leaving them out on the streets to be found.

Cheyenne was able to swing slightly. And a scream nearly escaped her despite her best efforts.

She had found the source of the dripping sound.

And she knew she wasn't just being held.

She was in line.

A woman was suspended by her ankles next to her. She had been hung upside down, her throat punctured.

And her life's blood was dripping, dripping into a pail that rested beneath her.

Cheyenne closed her eyes against the sight.

Andre will come, Andre will come…

She couldn't wonder if he'd be able to follow her trail. She had to believe that he would. They had been serious and worried when they planned to come here, but were certain such a bizarre case could be solved quickly. After, they planned to take a wickedly romantic vacation, perhaps in Scotland or down in Italy, or maybe even on the French Riviera or in Andalusia.

That concept wasn't looking quite so possible at the moment.

Had it been only days ago that they'd arrived at Highgate, just before Halloween? She could remember Emily's first hysterical call and how they had come to be here, what they had discovered, and what they had not.

Panic seized her, along with the pain that wracked her arms and head.

She fought it. She had to stay calm and determined.

Soon, she was. There had to be a way out.

And she would find it before she ever let the wretched *Vampire* of Highgate add another victim to his toll.

Think back! she told herself.

The answers to her escape might well be in the memories of the steps they had taken that had caused her to end up where she was now.

So, first…The call from Emily that had brought them across the Atlantic.

Chapter 1

"A cemetery? You want to visit another cemetery? Because of a murder?" Andre asked Cheyenne.

She stood at the counter in the apartment they'd just rented together in Alexandria, Virginia, and he couldn't help but be reminded of the great day they'd had thus far. This morning, they'd brought in the last of their belongings, including their suitcases since they'd returned from Louisiana to make their cohabitation arrangements and had been living out of a hotel room.

The apartment was terrific—a beautiful kitchen with modern appliances plus upgraded bathrooms—and yet the building itself was early Victorian, one on a street of historic row houses.

They loved it. And since they both had apartments in the D.C. area but had been busy moving things out of those and then in together, they'd opted for the ease of a hotel during the transition. Now, at last, they had a few days of leisure before returning to work.

Cheyenne had been with the FBI previous to meeting Andre—or re-meeting him—in Louisiana. They'd been on a strange case that had delved into both Cheyenne's and Andre's pasts. Now, she had been transferred to the Krewe, as well. They had taken down a particularly heinous killer, and that called for a few days' reprieve from the office.

Time enough to get into their new apartment.

The master bath boasted a fabulous Jacuzzi. They'd emerged from it recently, and while Cheyenne delivered information regarding her recent phone call, she stood in a big, white, fluffy towel.

Andre also wore a towel. He hadn't expected the conversation to go in this direction. She'd hopped up because she heard her cousin, Emily, on the answering machine and wanted to let her know that she'd call her back.

"We have time!" she whispered.

"To go to England?"

"She's my cousin," Cheyenne said. "And this is looking very bad for her."

Cousin…Cheyenne cannot lose another cousin.

Still. Emily lived in England.

"Cheyenne, we're Krewe, but that's still FBI. We don't have any authority or power in London or Highgate." He paused. "Is Highgate just the cemetery, or is it a town?"

"It's a cemetery and a suburban area of north London," Cheyenne said. She stared at him with wide eyes full of hope.

She had the most unusual eyes. They weren't brown. And they weren't green or blue. Instead, they had facets of both green and blue that grew more pronounced depending on her mood rather than any color she might be wearing. They could appear like the sky at times. At other times, they burned as gold as any fire.

She was going, he knew. Whether he did or not.

He hesitated. Their recent case had revolved around a cemetery, too.

And was a replay back to old murders, with one of the victims having been Cheyenne's cousin.

"All right."

"All right?"

"Of course. Your cousin is in trouble. We will have no power or authority, but we can be there to give her emotional strength and help her figure out what's going on and… What *is* going on?" he asked.

"A vampire seems to be behind it," she said.

"A vampire?"

The Krewe of Hunters were members of an unusual unit of the bureau. They had the unique ability to speak to the dead who remained behind, those who chose to communicate with the living.

But vampires?

"A murderer," she said quietly. "One who is choosing to revitalize the story of the Vampire of Highgate, leaving a trail of dead. One of those victims was found on Emily's front porch."

"Ah, um, ah," he said. "Okay, so…we'll see who Adam Harrison might know over there and if he can help us any with local authorities." Adam was the Krewe's founder, a man as well known for his diplomatic and charitable achievements as he was for his work with the bureau. An amazing man. Still…

Highgate. Andre was sure it was a lovely town. But they were American. And the crimes were being committed in England.

And, no pun intended, even to himself, he was sick to death of cemeteries.

"You'll have to bring me up to date on the old legends of the Highgate vampire."

She nodded solemnly. "We'll both go? Really?"

"Really. Of course."

She smiled and flew across the distance that separated them, straight into his arms. Her towel fell to the floor along the way. When she leapt into his arms, his towel dropped, too.

The night was going to be all right, after all.

But come the morning…

He wasn't going to think about the morning right now. He was just going to breathe in the scent of her and feel the silk of her skin and hair…

And watch that beautiful, burning golden light that came into her eyes when they made love.

* * * *

"Media," Andre said, glancing at Cheyenne. "So, reading up, here's what I see. There was an incident at Tottenham Park Cemetery in London in 1968. Very weird things were done. Vandalism, but with bones and flowers. One grave was dug up, the coffin opened, and the body in it staked through the heart. Right after that, various people began seeing things at Highgate Cemetery: a lady in white, a ghostly cyclist, and a man in a top hat with a ghastly face—obviously a vampire. So, in the sixties, the cemetery was already over a hundred years old, overgrown and in terrible disrepair. The first sighting of the vampire was by a couple walking down Swain's Lane. The stories grew, and two figures back then became notable. Men named David Farrant and Sean Manchester. The first, it seems to me, was a rather harmless spiritualist who caused the flurry. The second considered himself a bishop in a church of his own creation. He came up with a story that the vampire was from Romania, had known Vlad the Impaler—*the* Dracula—and somehow wound up buried there, hundreds of years before Highgate came into existence. Manchester claimed the vampire had been awakened by Satanists."

Cheyenne nodded with a grimace. "Yes, legends allow for a lot, right? There was a real frenzy back then from what I understand. People became desperate to stop the vampire by breaking the gates, desecrating tombs. All that and more."

"In 1971, a headless, charred body with a stake through its heart was found in the cemetery," Andre noted. "And, according to a book by Manchester, he stalked the vampire for thirteen years, found it, staked it, and killed it. But then his companion, Luisa, was taken over by the vampire. She turned into a giant spider, and he staked her, too."

"Thing is, as with any legend, people will see what they choose to see."

"And crazies will help them see things," he murmured. "That was the past. This is the present." He glanced at her again, glad that talking was easy enough on their long flight.

Adam hadn't just approved their trip, he'd managed to get them a great flight in the business section of a 787 Dreamliner.

It was nice, and Andre was grateful. He knew Cheyenne was still amazed. While being in the Krewe sometimes drew ridicule, it had its perks, too. And even those who ridiculed had to begrudgingly acknowledge the Krewe's statistics for solving unsolvable cases.

Few, of course, would believe why.

"So, to today…while none of the bodies have been found in the cemetery, they've been found close by. And thus, the legend of the vampire has risen again," he said.

He was somber as he spoke. The police didn't buy the concept that a vampire had returned to Highgate. Not officially—and probably not at all.

There were three dead. The first, Vanessa Lark, had been found at one end of Swain's Lane, draped over a bench, white as a sheet and, as the medical examiner would soon discover, drained of blood.

The second, Olivia Wordsworth, had been found at the other end of the lane, leaning atop a stone plaque, also exsanguinated.

The third and most recent had been found on the steps of Emily Donegal's small entry porch. Eric Morton, her fiancé, had been questioned relentlessly, and Emily had been brought in for questioning, as well, right before her frantic call to Cheyenne. The third victim had been identified as Sheila Marie Lynsey, and she had once dated Eric Morton. They had, in fact, been involved for several years before they split up two years ago.

When the two were together, Sheila had lived with Eric in the house on Swain's Lane.

"The murderer returning Ms. Lynsey's body to her previous home...sickly poetic," Andre murmured.

"Just sick," Cheyenne said. "Andre, you don't think someone killed the other women just to put a vampire spin on it all before getting to Sheila Lynsey, do you? Trying to make Eric look guilty? Or Emily? It sounds like they questioned my cousin, thinking she could be guilty of this because she was jealous or afraid of Sheila."

"Admit it, we'd have to take a look at that possibility, too," Andre said.

"You haven't met Emily yet," Cheyenne said. "She's sweet, tiny, fragile. She moved to London about four years ago because she was working in customer service for the hotel business, and her company transferred her over. Because she's so sweet, she can usually soothe even the most enraged customer. But she has a good head on her shoulders and can solve situations with both the hotel and the customer, delivering the best solution to any discord."

"And Eric? You know him?"

Cheyenne nodded. "He's a translator. He speaks four languages fluently and has been hired to translate books from Spanish, Italian, and French into English. His mom was Norse, and so, while I'd call him fluent in Norwegian, as well, he says he's not completely proficient in the language and won't offer his services in it. His dad was a professor at Oxford. But he's tall, and I guess that means he could pop on a hat and grab a cane and be a vampire... I don't know. It was the last victim that caused the police to look at the two of them. The thing is, Andre, it's likely that whoever this killer is, he knew about Eric's past and that he'd be a suspect. And Emily...she could be a person of interest. Or if they're trying to nail Eric, a victim."

Andre reclined his seat and looked over at Cheyenne.

"Try to get some sleep. It's going to be a very long day. And night," he surmised.

She leaned back.

He caught her hand—not easy over the divide—and squeezed it.

This killer was playing off the legend and the past.

A headless, charred corpse with a stake through its heart had been found on a long-ago Halloween.

And the last day of October was fast approaching.

They were going to have to discover the truth quickly. Because Andre was in no way convinced this killer was a vampire.

Just a very clever murderer. One with an agenda.

And that plan might well include Emily.

Chapter 2

Eric's house was on the steep end of Swain's Lane. His Victorian home was just down from a modern housing complex, complete with glass and chrome—and, Cheyenne thought, every possible modern convenience.

She'd let Emily know when they landed, and while Emily had offered to pick them up, Andre had wanted to rent a car. She'd been somewhat nervous about either of them driving on what they saw as the "wrong" side of the road, but Andre quickly proved adept at changing lanes. When she glanced his way, he shrugged and said, "Yeah, I've done this before. But last time, it was for a vacation."

"Well, we can think of this as a strange holiday. Tourists do come to visit Highgate. It's considered a microcosm of Victorian art and ideals. The cemetery is beautiful, and there are a lot more controls in place now than there were forty to sixty years ago."

They arrived at Emily and Eric's. As her cousin had assured her, there was just enough space on the side of the old house for the little car they had rented.

Emily quickly came out onto the small porch that led to the residence. Just three steps and perhaps three or four feet of brick. Cheyenne glanced up as they arrived. The home had two floors and an attic, two charming towers, dormers, and turrets. It was lovely and painted a soft bluish-gray. The porch wasn't wide but wrapped around the structure, and the house had many windows.

Emily appeared especially tiny against the rise of the façade, though the building wasn't at all huge. She had a soft shade of hair much like

Cheyenne's, and pale green eyes.

Her delicate face showed signs of the strain she'd been enduring.

"Cheyenne!"

She raced down the steps to throw her arms around Cheyenne and hold her tight. For a moment, Cheyenne lost her breath. She hugged her cousin fiercely in return.

Emily began to babble. "I'm so sorry, I know I shouldn't have asked you to come. Eric says that I shouldn't have. I mean, thinking back on Janine and her murder and the killer and what you've just been through…"

"Emily, I'm an FBI agent. That's what I do—deal with the bad."

"Because of what happened to Janine," Emily murmured.

"Yes, but what we do is important. You called me. If you hadn't, I'd have come anyway and…"

She paused. Emily was staring at Andre, and Cheyenne managed to smile and step back to draw him closer.

"Emily, Andre. Andre, Emily."

"Pleasure to meet you, Emily," Andre said. "Though I wish the circumstances were different."

Emily nodded, pumped his hand in greeting, then looked at Cheyenne. "He's gorgeous!" she said. "Oh, sorry, come in, come in, please. They took the crime scene tape down early this morning, thank God. We can come and go through our front door again, but that means nothing given the dead woman on our steps. And, poor Eric! He's so distressed. He and Sheila didn't break up badly, contrary to what everyone seems to think. Well, except for those who want to think they were still in love." She shook her head.

"And, obviously, I must be a monster of a person, killing two women to make it look like a would-be vampire is doing it. Oh! Of course, there are those in the area who *do* believe the vampire has come back. People are sneaking into the cemetery at night, carrying out more Satanic rites, raising the dead—vampires among them. But come in. Come in, please!"

Cheyenne couldn't help but inwardly grin at her cousin's ramble. Emily kept Cheyenne's hand as they reached the porch. And as they headed up the steps, Eric appeared in the doorway.

Cheyenne had learned through her years in criminology and as an agent, that killers didn't have a particular *look*. Some were obviously a little demented; others, like Ted Bundy, were capable of such charm that they could far too easily lure unwary victims into their clutches.

But if she were to pick someone who *didn't* look like a killer, it would be Eric Morton.

Eric loved books, reading, languages, and history. He was a fairly tall man at about six feet, but like Emily, he was very thin. He wore soda-bottle thick glasses, had scruffy, short-cropped blond hair, and powder blue eyes that looked as if they belonged on the most innocent babe. And he was always quick to smile.

Again, like Emily, he tended to be naïve and look for the good in others. Someone could repeatedly stab him in the back metaphorically, and he'd be oblivious to the fact.

Today, however, he didn't appear ignorant. He looked tired and worn and far older than his thirty-eight years. He smiled when he saw Cheyenne, though, extending welcoming arms.

She accepted his hug, introducing Andre as she did, and the men shook hands.

"In, in, in!" Emily said. "Trust me. They're watching us from the new high-rise, and the damned walls seem to watch you these days. Oh, don't get me wrong, I love Highgate. But…"

"These are very strange times," Eric said.

"Tea. We have tea on. Oh, dear. I've been in England a long time now. I should have made coffee," Emily murmured.

"Tea is great," Andre told her.

They were soon seated in the expansive kitchen, one that had probably been upgraded about a decade ago. It had little bits of charm such as a brick wall to one side, and hanging copper pots and utensils. A large butcher block, probably almost as old as the house, was in the center, and they sat around it on carved wooden stools.

"Let's start right in, shall we?" Andre said. "What do the police think they have on you, Eric?"

Eric lifted his hands. "My relationship with Sheila, and the fact she was found on my steps," he said.

Cheyenne realized she loved to listen to him talk. He had a beautiful accent, clear and concise and yet…so wonderfully British.

"Did they accuse you outright?" Andre asked.

Eric shook his head. "No, they just brought us both in. Emily and me. And we went through my relationship with Sheila." His face clouded. "I lost a friend. We were still friends. We were just friends going in different directions. And she knew Emily. I believe she was even happy for me." He hesitated, glancing at Emily. "She felt I had found someone…as boringly rustic as myself."

"Charmed," Emily murmured and then shook her head. "I just can't believe this happened. I'm so, so sorry. Yes, we'd met, of course. Sheila lived closer to the center of London, but we met with a group of friends for dinner a couple of times, and she knew me. And I knew her. We laughed about our relationship being awkward and all, but…we were fine with one another."

"And you told all that to the police?" Cheyenne asked.

They both nodded.

"Okay, did you know either of the other young women who were killed?" Andre asked.

Both shook their heads, almost as one.

Andre looked at his notes. "The first woman was killed the first day of October, and the second on the thirteenth. History shows that Halloween is when all the sightings and whatnot begin. But, seriously, Halloween in England isn't like the crazy American event, right? Not until recently."

"From ancient times, it's been the night of the dead," Eric said. "Samhain, to the old Gaelic, celebrating the end of the light season of the year, and the beginning of the darkness. Also, the night when the veil between the living and the dead is weakest. I mean, seriously, yes, it became a big commercial holiday for you Yankees way before we had that kind of craziness here. But that doesn't mean people didn't celebrate the dead or the end of light and the beginning of darkness. They call it All Hallows' Eve because the following day is All Saints' Day." He paused, offering them a weak smile. "You Americans forget that so much in your culture came from us. I mean, where else would one find Puritans who ran for religious reasons and then hanged others for differing religions? We gave you crazy, my good bloke!"

"Well, having seen some episodes of *Benny Hill*," Andre told him, "I have no doubt you're not nearly as stoic, prim, or sane as we tend to think. But has Halloween become a bigger deal over here through the years?"

Emily and Eric looked at one another and then nodded.

"You saw decorations on the way in, I'm sure," Eric said.

"All right. What about suspects?" Andre asked.

"Well, they interviewed another whack job, like the chaps all those years ago who fueled the whole paranormal and vampire thing about the cemetery," Eric said.

"Fellow calls himself 'Father Faith,'" Emily told them. "He does readings, holds seances, that kind of thing. He got himself interviewed for the papers and claims that, yes, there is something in Highgate, it's never been stopped, and it's readying itself for something big on Halloween."

Andre's phone buzzed softly, and he rose and excused himself to answer it.

"Do you know where we can find Father Faith?" Cheyenne asked.

"Sure," Emily said. "He has an occult shop just down in the center of town."

"He'll have to wait," Andre said, coming to the table and pulling back Cheyenne's chair. "We have a meeting with Inspector Adair of Scotland Yard. Now."

She looked up at him questioningly at first, but then she knew.

Adam Harrison had somehow worked his magic from across the pond. They couldn't *officially* be on any kind of an investigation, but Adam had managed to get them the unofficial help that might change the playing field.

"But…you just got here," Emily said. "After a trans-Atlantic flight. Don't you need to rest, to eat, to…feel your feet on the ground?"

"No, we're fine. And the quicker we move…well, we're only five days from Halloween, aren't we? Got to move faster than a speeding bullet here."

"Superman," Eric said. "I do love American comics."

"Well, not Superman. Just human trying to do our best," Andre said. "And we need to get into Highgate."

"None of the bodies were found in the cemetery," Eric said.

"You love history as much as languages. Can you pull up some original maps, noting anything remarkable or with changes and get them to my email?" Andre asked.

"Sure. Be prepared for a hunk of email. But as I said, no one was killed in the cemetery. There are visiting hours now, and a lot more security on the place. Though there is still a lot of that old, charming decay thing going on, despite the historical value. One side—the east side—allows visitors to roam freely. That's where Karl Marx is buried with a giant head memorial. Once you're in the area, you can't miss it. The other side is by guided tour only."

"Great," Andre said. "We'll take a tour this afternoon. Then we'll see Father Faith. If you think of anything else, give us a call."

Andre quickly led Cheyenne out of the house and to the car.

"What?" she demanded, sliding into the passenger's seat. "Something else happened. You dragged me out of there so fast!"

"Another young woman has been reported missing," Andre said. He looked her way. "She was last seen walking down Swain's Lane in the vicinity of your cousin's home," he added softly. "We are going to have to find out what the hell is going on here and quickly. Because it's beginning to look as if someone wants your cousin or Eric either looking guilty as hell…or dead."

Chapter 3

Their meeting with Inspector Adair was at a coffee shop in the center of the main area of town.

Andre recognized him immediately, though he wasn't sure why. He was in plain clothes, a casual tweed suit with light brown trim, a matching vest, and a casual cap—much like a deerstalker.

He rose when he saw them. Evidently, they were just as obvious in their appearance as either an American couple on holiday or law enforcement agents with no authority in the U.K.

"Special Agents Donegal and Rousseau?" Inspector Adair asked, offering his hand. He was perhaps forty-five with light brown eyes and matching hair. His cheekbones were wide, and his smile was generous, giving him a pleasant look. But Cheyenne also noted that he seemed to have a jaw of steel.

"Yes, yes. And thank you so much for seeing us. We realize it's quite a favor," Cheyenne said, and Andre nodded in agreement.

"Please, sit down. I've taken the liberty of ordering coffee. I love the stuff. You know, we English and our tea-time… Give me coffee every day. Did you know we've had coffee longer than tea? They both arrived in the 1600s, but java came first—by about a decade. Now, you folks probably opted to go for coffee first because you were breaking away, but now we're all happy allies, so we can enjoy both!"

"Yes, we can," Andre said as they settled themselves at the table. "You're working this case as the main investigator by yourself?"

"Oh, no. But my partner, Inspector Claude Birmingham, suddenly found he had something else to do." Adair lowered his voice. "He's read up on the Krewe in America. Says we don't need any more hocus-pocus here." Frowning, he leaned back and regarded them. "I have also read up on the Krewe. And I don't give a bloody damn what you do if you can help. Occultists...paranormal experts...they're jumping out of the woodwork here. Ghosts are killing, vampires are murdering...and seances must be performed in the cemetery. It's crazy!"

"Someone human, of flesh and blood, is doing the killing," Andre said flatly. "I just spoke to my field director back home. He said he'd gotten word that another young woman has gone missing."

Adair's eyebrows rose briefly at the fact that they knew this information, but he quickly schooled his features and controlled his surprise.

"Yes," he admitted. "But we've just taken the initial report. Normally, we wouldn't be concerned. You know how missing persons reports go. The young woman's name is Edith Greenbriar. She was partying with friends and was last seen walking down Swain's Lane toward the home of the relatives she was staying with. Near your cousin's house, Miss—sorry, Special Agent Donegal."

"I'm not really a special anything here, am I?" Cheyenne replied easily with a wave of her hand. "We appreciate you talking to us at all."

Adair nodded solemnly, glancing between them with curiosity. "You're a couple? I mean, not just partners, but—*partners*?"

"Yes," Andre confirmed.

"Interesting."

Andre returned his gaze. "We were both with the bureau before we met," he said briefly. "Different units then."

Adair shrugged. "Who am I to judge?"

"Can you tell us about this young woman, Edith Greenbriar?" Cheyenne asked, leaning forward.

He nodded. "Pretty girl, twenty-three, bright-eyed, attractive blonde. She came down from York, lived near Westminster, but took the train up here often because of friends and distant relatives. She was with some of them, supposedly returning home to her family's place after a night out, and never showed up for work this morning. She's a sales assistant for a high-end clothing line. Sometimes, as we all know, young women take off. So do young men, of course. But with what's been going on here, we've decided to investigate immediately."

"Any leads?"

"Only, as I mentioned, that they saw her walk down Swain's Lane."

"And you talked to the residents at the new, high-priced apartments?" Andre asked.

"We did."

"One would think she might have been followed from there," Cheyenne observed.

"We're not discounting that. But—"

Andre raised his eyebrows. "But?"

"No bodies were found there," Adair said quietly. "Please, we are not making easy assumptions here. We have, as one says, persons of interest."

"And who are those people?" Cheyenne pressed.

Adair looked straight at her. "Your cousin and her boyfriend are among them."

Cheyenne knew not to get angry. Being angry just meant they would quit communicating. She focused on keeping her expression neutral. "Why?" she asked seriously. "Why focus on them and not your other suspects?"

"A bloodless body on their doorstep. Especially when that doorstep used to belong to the bloodless body," Adair clarified.

"You interviewed Emily and Eric," Andre pointed out. "And you searched the residence. Did you find anything that suggested they might be guilty of abducting and then draining the blood from three women?"

Adair ran a hand over his face. "No," he admitted. "And that's why they're not under arrest. We have nothing."

"But you have other persons of interest," Andre said.

Adair hesitated just a minute. "We do."

Cheyenne caught his gaze and held it. "But you're not willing to share that information?"

Again, Adair hesitated. "All right. You didn't get this from me," he said finally, in a lower voice. "We have a few. There's Clark Brighton, who lives in the new apartments near your cousin. He's a so-called spiritualist. *Spiritualist*, not psychic. Not sure about the difference." Adair shrugged, then rolled his eyes.

"He's in his mid-fifties, a loner, but has a cult-like following. He writes essays on the cures to be found in the air and through positive thought. He says there is a Satanic cult at work again. But he's all New Age love and hugs, or so it appears. He's an interesting character." Adair stopped to take a breath.

"The last young lady, your Sheila, was seeing a few men casually. She dated Mark Bower, a banker who lives just outside the village area. And Benjamin Turner, a local writer and media sensation. Does up bits of history from all over London. He has sponsors on his site and makes a decent living at it. But remember, please—"

"What about the friends Edith Greenbriar was visiting, or the family she was staying with?" Cheyenne interrupted.

"Patricia Franks and Victoria Mason. Distant relatives. Both are in their seventies and arthritic. And the other friends Edith had been out with that night don't know anything either," Adair said. "But yes, before you ask, she could have been followed from the building. Again, please, please, remember—"

"That we're not here to investigate officially, and that you didn't say a word to us," Cheyenne supplied with a grin.

Adair nodded. Their coffee arrived, and they enjoyed it while Adair shared a short history of the town and the surrounding area. He also told them he'd set them up with a private tour of the Highgate Cemetery for the afternoon.

"Mainly to the West Cemetery. That's guided tour only. Monte will meet you at the main gate in…" Inspector Adair paused to look at his watch. "In fifty-five minutes. And I, I will be at the autopsy. If you learn anything, I expect you'll inform me immediately, no matter who it involves."

"Of course," Cheyenne assured him.

They rose, thanked him for the coffee, and then Andre asked, "What about a man called Father Faith?"

"An idiot," Adair exclaimed, waving an arm impatiently in the air. "His shop is just a few stores down. He's a psychic, though how the hell people fall for all that shite, I do not know! Sorry. He sells incense, herbs, does palm readings, and all that rot. He's tall and dark and, I dare say, tries to look like a vampire himself. And, yes, we found him to be a person of interest immediately. Real name is William Smith. We couldn't find anything on him, though, other than him warning followers on his social media channels that they needed his special herbs and kits to protect against vampires." He gave a mirthless laugh.

"Had him staked out until our men tired of watching him buy milk and head home to bed. He's as big a creep as those magicians who caused the frenzy on October 13th in 1970. Hundreds jumping the fences with their stakes and all, doing irreparable damage. Coffins dumped and corpses staked… God save us from such lunatics." He paused. "Whoops, sorry. Even over here, there are rumors about your Krewe. You're not…um, weird like that, right?"

"No, we're not weird like that," Andre assured him with a chuckle.

Cheyenne couldn't help but respond. "Oh, no. We're weird in an entirely different way."

For a moment, Inspector Adair looked worried, but then he laughed. "Oh, aye, there you go, Americans kidding around. Great. Well, keep me informed of anything you find."

"We promise," Cheyenne said sweetly.

"And meet your guide—his name is Monte Bolton—at the main gate in"—he looked at his watch again—"fifty minutes now."

"Will do, and thank you," Andre said.

Adair waved and hurried out, pulling his hat back on.

"He's really all right, you know," Andre told Cheyenne as they watched the inspector leave.

She smiled. "Yes, he was a decent sort. But we are weird—in our way. So, on to the psychic?"

"On to the psychic," Andre agreed. "We now have forty-eight minutes."

* * * *

Given the time he'd spent in Salem, Massachusetts, and his time in New Orleans, Louisiana, Andre had met many a so-called psychic. Some seemed sincere, though he believed they simply had a talent for reading people and telling them things they might already know.

Most were shams.

Father Faith—or William Smith—fell into the latter grouping, Andre decided, though that quick assessment might not be fair. He knew witches in Salem who were really Wiccans, respecting their faith as a religion. He knew some who were all show for the tourists who came into their shops, fascinated and ready to drop their dollars.

It was the same in New Orleans. There were very good voodoo practitioners and priests and priestesses. But he knew those who were total con artists, too.

In both *alternative* religions, no harm was to be done to others. Harm done came back on the one who attempted it. Both Hollywood—and Doc Duvalier in Haiti—had given voodoo a very bad name.

The shop they approached was called *Father Faith's*.

"How original," Cheyenne deadpanned, and he shot her a smile as he opened the door.

Andre hadn't needed to get inside to perform his initial assessment of the man. His first impression had come from the front window, which displayed modern *vampire kits*, bottles of potions made from garlic, "*guaranteed to drive away vampires and other forces of evil*," plus all manner of sterling jewelry, from crosses to earrings and more.

Father Faith seemed to be a focal point of the store himself. He stood talking to a customer and gesturing to the shelves that offered all sorts of arcane items: stakes, vials of garlic, oils, candles, herbs, talismans, tarot cards, books, and crosses in wood or silver of varying sizes and all price points.

As Inspector Adair had told them, William Smith was a tall man, dark-haired, and could easily have been cast as a vampire in any movie. His shoulders were broad, and his age was difficult to determine. But however old he might be—somewhere between forty-five to maybe even sixty—he was extremely fit, moved fluidly, and carried himself with an air of drama and confidence. His eyes were dark, his face was pale, and he wore a collar that seemed not quite priestly, but very close to it.

Cheyenne and Andre pretended interest in a rack of jewelry, a lot of it beautifully crafted. Father Faith might be a psychic, but he was also good at acquisitions.

There was a curtain at the back wall of the shop by the cash register, with a sign that alerted the customers that there was a place for private sessions. Presumably those palm readings the inspector had mentioned.

The man with whom William Smith had been talking made his purchase and left the store—thanking Smith profusely.

When they approached him where he stood behind the cash register, the man set the back of his hand theatrically to his forehead.

"I know who you are!" he proclaimed in a dramatic tone.

"You do?" Andre inquired politely.

"Americans," Smith said as if it were an accusation.

"That we are."

Father Faith set both hands on the counter, shaking his head. "You're here because of the dreadful situation going on. I'm afraid more will fall into grave danger. Because—forgive me, I don't wish to be offensive—people come here fascinated by the malevolence that lurks, brought to life by…evil people."

"I definitely believe in evil people," Andre agreed.

"The police need to be looking for Satanists," Smith continued as if Andre hadn't spoken. "They bring evil unto the Earth."

"How do they recognize a Satanist when they see one?" Cheyenne asked.

His gaze shifting dramatically in her direction, Smith pointed two fingers toward her and then toward his own eyes. "You look deep," he said. "There's something back there. Something that gleams. That shows a communion with the devil."

Cheyenne gasped as if enthralled. "You really believe a vampire has been raised from the dead?"

He regarded her solemnly. "I never deny possibilities. Very bad things are happening here. *Have* happened. Seriously, dear lovely lady, this is not a good time for Americans to be in London—at Highgate."

"Thank you for the warning," Cheyenne said. She smiled and gestured to the shelves. "Well, what do I need to protect myself?"

Smith glanced at Andre as if waiting for approval.

"Everyone should be protected." Andre nodded.

William Smith hustled to retrieve several of his kits, laying them out on the counter and describing the different components and their uses— as he had done with the customer before them.

Everything was outrageously expensive, but Cheyenne didn't say so.

She listened intently, nodding and frowning in concentration.

"I'll have to think on this," she said finally when he finished his spiel and turned to watch her expectantly. "That's…well, frankly, a lot of travel money."

"Think on it," he said. Then he reached inside one of the kits. "This. I insist you take. From me. A welcome gift to our friends from across the pond."

It was a silver necklace.

Cheyenne demurred. "I'm sorry. I can't take anything so valuable."

Smith placed it on the counter and shook his head. "It looks like silver, but it's a cheap metal. And it will last for your stay here, I believe. Pull the lower section of the cross."

Glancing at Andre, she picked it up and did as Smith requested. The lower portion of the cross separated to reveal a small but sharp dagger.

Smith returned to his Father Faith persona, more mystic than shopkeeper. "It just might save your life."

"I—"

"Oh, take it, Special Agent Donegal," he said, causing her to arch her brows.

He smiled. "I'm friends with Inspector Claude Birmingham, Inspector Michael Adair's partner. Birmingham considers the two of you to be a bit daft and didn't want to meet with you. I told him it would be his bloody loss, but the bugger is a bit of a prig, you know. Knocks my shop, but I do quite well here. Ah, and he'll leave you be. Much as he mocks me, he's still my friend. I knew you'd show up. Please, do take this little gadget, Special Agent Donegal. A sign we've long ago forgiven that whole Revolution thing, you know?"

She smiled. "Sure. And thank you."

"If it's quite all right with you, sir," he inquired of Andre.

Andre shrugged. "Cheyenne makes her own decisions in all things. But it's a lovely gesture. *If* she wants my opinion."

"Brilliant. Then be off, my new friends. I believe you have a tour coming up."

They thanked Smith and left the shop.

"What do you think?" Cheyenne asked.

"I think it's an interesting gadget. And you never know, that's a pretty damned sharp little blade. It could come in handy."

"I mean about the man."

"Well, I know I don't like Birmingham."

"We don't know him."

"It wasn't his place to tell others what we were doing."

"Ah. Maybe he thinks we need looking after."

"I don't know. I don't like it. Anyway, we've got three minutes. We need to hurry down the lane. I think the main entry is ahead."

And it was. Huge, stark, and in Gothic decay despite revitalization, the main entry awaited them. They rushed ahead, ready to meet their guide.

And enter the Highgate realm of the dead.

Chapter 4

Cheyenne quickly determined that Monte Bolton was a good guide. From the start, he seemed eager to meet them, curious, friendly, and ready to answer any questions.

He was in his early forties but moved with the agility and enthusiasm of a much younger man and was obviously very knowledgeable.

Cheyenne immediately liked him and his easy manner.

He wore a simple tailored shirt and jeans, brushing a lock of sandy hair from his forehead before they shook hands.

"I hear you two are intrigued. And I'm impressed," he gushed. "You're from Louisiana, right? They have quite amazing cemeteries there, as well, yes? Cities of the Dead! One day, I'll get there."

"Yes, we're from Louisiana, but we live in D.C. now," Andre told him. "And this...well, it's huge, for one. And the landscaping...remarkable."

"So many buried here," Monte told him. "You don't mind walking, do you?"

"Not at all," Cheyenne assured him. "We're grateful to you."

"Not a problem. My, uh, cousin asked me to do this," he said.

"Your cousin?" Andre asked.

"Inspector Michael Adair." Monte lowered his voice slightly, though there was no one around to hear.

"He and old Birmingham get along all right, but Mike thinks Birmingham is being a wanker. There's no reason you shouldn't be here—and helping if possible. So, cousin Mikey called to make sure I gave you the old A-1 tour. And I hope to!"

"We're sure you will."

"The stakes are high for me, eh? I mean, you come from Louisiana. I've seen pictures and have read up on some of your places. Fantastic." Again, he lowered his voice. "And this Krewe thing of yours...it's intriguing. Do you really solve just about everything?"

"We try our hardest," Cheyenne said.

"Deep, dark secrets of the investigations?" he asked.

"We go through the academy. We work all hours of the day. Pretty much like any law enforcement officers," Andre said.

They headed through the cemetery, Monte pointing out various *special* graves, either because of the person buried there or the funerary art.

One grave with an obelisk marker set by a stunning weeping angel, caught Cheyenne's attention. The epitaph was beautiful.

Here lies she in beauty and grace,
Kind in soul and gentle in face,
And surely now with angels she soars,
Watching over all she adores,
For goodness ruled her every breath
Stolen so cruelly, unto death.
Oh, bitter loss, while we shed tears
Let her killer know new fears
For in Heaven she will gently tread
Eternal, while flames shall fill the other with dread.

"Lovely, and so sad! I'm taking this to mean she was murdered?" she asked softly, thinking Andre was still at her side. But he was a bit away, studying a small mausoleum tomb created in the Egyptian style.

She thought he looked at the tomb but also...

Beyond it.

Monte was talking and moving ahead. "See the cherubs? Several children are buried here. There was a time in London when four out of five children died at tender ages."

Cheyenne and Andre looked at one another and smiled. Their guide assumed they were still with him, so they hurried to catch up.

Art was plentiful, diverse, and fantastic in the cemetery. There were various styles of monuments such as pianos and other instruments, those that celebrated pets and animals and, of course, weeping angels, life-size Christ statues, and children with lambs. Many graves were merely headstones, but others were so much more.

"The owners of the cemetery could no longer maintain it back in 1975, so it was closed, and the gates were locked. But, eventually, the

Friends of Highgate Cemetery took over and did a tremendous amount of work restoring what they could. Imagine first the ground. It rises and falls. Over time, it shifts naturally. Trees and underbrush take over. But a good deal of work has preserved much of what was," Monte informed them as they moved.

"It's a beautiful place," Cheyenne observed.

"Yes, it follows the concept of a garden cemetery. First, think back to Christian history. Burials were customarily done in churchyards, but then populations soared, and space became scarce. In England, entrepreneurs created private burial grounds, but corruption was rampant, coffins were re-used, and bodies were dumped. And, of course," Monte said, "there were ghouls who stole bodies to sell to medical schools and then took to creating their own corpses—à la the infamous Scots, Burke and Hare! Now, the great architect—and scholar, astrologist, mathematician, and so on—Sir Christopher Wren, was ahead of his time. In the 1600s, he stated that cemeteries should be at the city limits. But after people started to complain—especially after fever outbreaks—that it was terribly unhealthy and that the dead were killing the living, the idea became far more mainstream. It took a few hundred years, more increases in population, fevers, and so on, but the great Victorian cemeteries sprung up around London. Highgate opened in 1839. There are in-ground burial spots, tombs, small family mausoleums, huge family crypts, catacombs, statues, monuments, and more."

He stopped and spread out his arms, indicating the area where they now stood. "There is nothing else in the world like this. The Circle of Lebanon. These magnificent—or magnificently creepy—catacombs we see here, allowed for families to be together. Or individuals to be buried. The Egyptian thing—some people wanted their remains to be above ground. Remember, the Victorians were fascinated by all things Egyptian, so you have Egyptian Avenue, the beautiful arch, the chapel, and so much more. But there are so many types of graves and tombs and mausoleums and catacombs here. Approximately one hundred and seventy thousand people rest here, in fifty-three thousand graves."

The catacombs or mausoleum that they now entered was fascinating. Coffins lined some shelves, but others were empty. Some were sealed, and some were not. Some lids were broken and hung at odd angles.

"They had an interesting problem here," Monte continued as they wandered through the crypt. "Victorians believed that *death gasses* caused disease. And, so, being interred here meant being in a lead-lined coffin.

But gasses built up, and they had a problem with exploding coffins. They solved that with pin holes that allowed a small bit of gas to escape, bit by bit, and small fires were lit to destroy the gasses during the first weeks."

He stopped speaking. "Beautiful and sad. Especially here. You must remember, while restoration efforts have been massive, some things were lost." He shrugged. "Relatives, for one. Sometimes, there are no descendants to worry about the bodies of loved ones and…coffins break, remains are lost, stones shift. Well, you've seen the terrain here. Underground, above ground, things change. That's nature. And, as you know, Swain's Lane is steep!"

"Very," Andre agreed.

They emerged into daylight once again. "I can only imagine what it was like in the 1960s and 1970s before the Friends of Highgate Cemetery stepped in. There's footage, of course, of the insanity when the vampire scare hit its peak, and people rushed the place by the scores, hopping the gates with their vampire-killing kits!"

He'd been grinning, but his smile faded. He looked at them, intensity in his eyes.

"I guess someone is playing vampire again, in a bloody horrid way."

"Yes," Cheyenne murmured.

"Any ideas? I mean, you don't think a *real* vampire like old Count Dracula has truly awakened within the cemetery, do you? What with you being with the Krewe of Hunters and all."

"We're more into the concept that someone might like to play at being a vampire, or make it appear as if the old legend might be true," Cheyenne said.

"No deep thoughts on it?"

"We've barely gotten started here," Andre said. "But, again, we thank you. It's good to visit the cemetery the vampire was known to haunt years ago—and is supposedly haunting again."

Monte remained silent for a few minutes as if waiting for one of them to speak again, or ruminating on a question of his own.

"Well," he said at last, "I'll get you back. Oh, just so you know, it's still a working cemetery, should you want a plot to investigate. They close down sometimes for funerals. And even where you must be with someone like me, if you have a loved one buried here, you can get a pass to…uh, visit them without the benefit of a guide."

"Interesting," Andre said.

"Now, you're welcome to wander the other side," Monte said. "Until closing. That will be at five this afternoon. But you need to see Karl Marx. His monument is a giant head!"

He led them back. Cheyenne wasn't sure what Andre wanted to do. She was pretty sure that seeing the grave of Karl Marx—giant head or no—wouldn't be the most important part of their day.

Turned out he did want to wander the east side of the cemetery.

They had just started off on their own when Andre said, "He's following us."

"Monte?"

"Let's lose him."

They did. Thankfully, the winding paths, trails, tombs, and overgrowth of the cemetery allowed them leeway to shake the man.

"Interesting character," Andre said.

"Suspect?" Cheyenne asked.

"I don't know, but something was a bit off. Anyway…he's not lurking behind us anymore, so we need to take up position somewhere."

"Huh?"

"Didn't you see her?"

"Her? Who?"

"I don't know *who*," he said. "A woman. About thirty or thirty-five. Attractive, Victorian attire, blue dress, white lace."

"No," Cheyenne said. "But if she was on the other side of the cemetery—"

"I think she saw us and noted I saw her, as well. And I believe she started following us. There aren't people ahead. Let's take that path and head deeper in. She seems curious about us and might want—and be able to—talk with us."

"All right."

They took a path that led through a row of small family tombs, perhaps housing six to ten coffins each. The architecture of the mausoleums was gracefully Gothic. The structures surrounded by overgrown brush with trees here and there throughout the area.

They stood alone by one of the elegant, gated buildings and waited.

A moment later, Cheyenne saw her.

Whoever she was, she'd been beautiful in life, and had died long before that beauty faded.

She seemed shy and hesitant but also eager to reach them. She paused just once in the path and then came their way.

"Hello?" the woman said softly.

"Hello," Cheyenne replied.

"You *do* see me. Hear me." She smiled. "So very rare! I see people shiver when I'm near. And one young man...well, I was quite sorry. I believe I terrified him, and that was not my intent. The passage of time is so different for me now. But it has been years I believe since I have been gifted enough to find those with this particular sight."

"I'm Andre Rousseau, and this is Cheyenne Donegal," Andre said politely, giving the ghost a slight bow. "And, yes, we both see and hear you clearly."

"Elizabeth Miller," she said. "I am delighted to make your acquaintance."

Cheyenne gasped softly. "Of course!" She thought of the epitaph she had read. She'd been so taken by the words that she had barely noted the name. But, yes, it had been Elizabeth. Elizabeth Miller.

"I saw your tomb on the other side of the cemetery. I'm so sorry. You died young—oh!" She fell silent, remembering the inscription on the tomb.

"Yes?"

"Life was...stolen from you. You were murdered," Cheyenne finished softly. "I am so sorry!"

"It was 1855," Elizabeth said. "But, please, don't look so stricken. My dear husband lay dead of a fever, and his sister lost her senses, striking out at me. I forgave her. She was not in her right mind. It was long ago, and I'm not at all vengeful. I don't usually haunt these decaying grounds. I have always enjoyed watching the street life in Highgate. Modern life goes on, while there remains a bit of respect for the past. Perhaps because of the culture retained in these old stones." She smiled. "I left behind five children. My descendants come here to this day when their time comes, and I often help them move on. And I watch. Perhaps I have stayed to save another from my fate. But it seems I have failed quite miserably in that as young women have died —and I was not able to help them."

"And still, you stay," Andre said.

"I was well known for my hospitality and my care of others, particularly my peers and the poor," she said lightly. "And, as I said, I like to believe the time will come when I can help. I may have failed thus far, but these killings will go on. And maybe, just maybe..."

"I am sure you will help," Cheyenne murmured. "*Lady* Miller. There was a larger obelisk. I didn't have time to read it, but I believe it was to...your husband and you, as well as other family members."

Elizabeth inclined her head. "I was born nobility—my father was an earl—and married into it as well...as was fitting in my day. Though, truly, perhaps I have also stayed to see more. Marriage between parties of all colors, choices...it was quite sad when so many things were not acceptable. When love was not acknowledged unless it was with the right class and the right color and the right sex."

"We still strive to move forward," Andre said, smiling. It was evident that Lady Miller had done her proper duty in life. But it appeared that, somewhere during her days on Earth, she might have been in love with someone she wasn't allowed to be with.

"Ah, yes. So, delightfully, here we three are! You're not screaming or fainting or weeping to someone around you that you're about to have the vapors. It's...not common. And again, so delightful. Now, most obviously, you are American."

"Most obviously, it seems," Cheyenne agreed with a smile.

"There's something about you..." Elizabeth murmured, "that leads me to believe you are here for a purpose. And I heard your guide telling you that his cousin, the inspector, arranged for your tour here today."

"We are law enforcement officers in the States," Andre said.

"And here to help *my* cousin," Cheyenne continued. "I believe she's in danger. Or that she and her boyfriend are being set up so they appear to be killers."

"Ah," Elizabeth murmured.

"Our guide, Monte. Have you seen him before?" Andre asked suddenly.

Elizabeth seemed thoughtful and then shrugged with a sweet smile. Cheyenne believed the woman must have been truly amazing in life—born to nobility, perhaps, but not bred to elitism. She was probably kind to everyone around her.

"I might have, I'm not sure. Not as a guide, though. Curious. But I'm not always watching or roaming where a guide might be. While I am most proud of my heritage and my country, I have heard tour guides many times. And not to be rude or cruel in any way, but the tours can be...a bit boring after a time."

"Of course," Cheyenne murmured. "Elizabeth, none of the bodies have been found here, but the killer has obviously been playing with the concept of the Highgate Cemetery. Do you believe he comes here, or is he just using the legend?"

Elizabeth smiled. "In the sixties and seventies—nineteen sixties and nineteen seventies, that is—the cemetery fell into serious disrepair. It was overgrown and not at all maintained. Today, of course, things are quite different."

"So, while an individual or a cult might have slipped in and out easily years ago, it's a bit different now. The killer is playing off a legend," Andre mused.

"The murders...most horrible!" Elizabeth said. "I've often wondered if one so cruelly taken from life might stay as I did. But if so, I have not seen them. Oh, I don't mean just here. I move beyond these confines occasionally. But while I love this precious chance to speak with the living, I followed you for a reason."

"Because you know something? You've seen something?" Andre asked, his handsome features sharp with hope and intensity.

"Nothing truly helpful, I'm afraid. To my sorrow. But there is something strange happening that has plagued me since it all started. I'm not sure what it means."

"Dear lady, please, what? We are grateful for any information," Andre said.

Elizabeth hesitated. "I have heard screams. Or cries...desperate sounds. I'm not sure..."

"From where?" Andre asked.

The ghost looked perplexed. "As I said, I'm not sure. It's like...like a moan from the earth."

"Here, in the cemetery?" Cheyenne asked.

"No, I don't believe so. But there's something like a tremor, an echo of sound. I've tried to trace the source, and all I'm certain of is that it is coming from the earth. Yet it seems to originate just north. On Swain's Lane, but...beyond the cemetery."

They were all silent for a moment.

Then Andre said, "Thank you, Lady Miller. Thank you, sincerely."

"Indeed, thank you," Cheyenne said softly.

"I will watch and listen and seek the advice of others who roam here," Elizabeth promised them. "I will listen for the moans from the earth. And I will follow them."

Cheyenne wished she could put her arms around the woman. She seemed strong yet one in need of comforting.

"Be careful," Cheyenne whispered.

Lady Elizabeth smiled. "What have I got to lose, dear friend? What have I got to lose?"

Chapter 5

With the cemetery closing, Andre and Cheyenne headed back out to Swain's Lane. Andre glanced at Cheyenne. She seemed so saddened by their meeting with Elizabeth Miller. She caught him watching her and smiled.

"Sorry, she was just so lovely…understanding illness, knowing what it's like to forgive. I'm not sure I could do it. And it's incredible she remains for her family. I suppose she hopes the time will come when she can keep her fate from befalling another."

"She just might, you know."

"The earth is crying," Cheyenne murmured. "She hears screams or moans. But," she paused, a frown knitting her brow, "wouldn't the living hear, as well?"

"Yes, but since the cemetery is known to be haunted, and half the world's population now thinks of themselves as paranormal researchers, you can find dozens of social media sites with people who claim to have met ghosts here. And those who say they've seen the vampire. Trying to determine what might be real and what's not is going to be quite a feat. Now, our good friend Inspector-slash-cousin Mikey might be able to find a way for us to search more of the underground cemetery. But I don't think his partner, Birmingham, is going to allow it. He doesn't want us here at all."

"That's it," Cheyenne said. "This killer is kidnapping his victims and taking them into a vault or somewhere underground. The very geographical structure here clearly allows for all manner of hidden vaults or tombs—or underground lairs!"

"Yes."

"So, what do we do?" Cheyenne asked, looking frustrated.

He smiled, pausing and turning to take her by the shoulders to pull her to him. He lifted her chin. "We figure it out. We need to regroup. I'm going to call Jackson and tell him another young woman is missing, and time is of the essence. Maybe Adam has a few more rabbits he can pull out of his hat. While we're waiting, we have a few more persons of interest to meet. And we took a long, long flight, got here at the crack of dawn, and have been going ever since. I'm going to suggest dinner with your cousin and Eric, and then procedure. We need to organize what we do and do not know and make a plan for moving forward."

"Procedure, of course," she said, smiling at him.

He remembered how they had met—or re-met—not so long ago. She had lost Janine when she was young, and he knew now that Janine's funeral had been Cheyenne's introduction to those who remained. While he'd barely seen Cheyenne at the time, her cries for her cousin had led to the murderer's capture and to Cheyenne becoming an FBI agent.

Years later, a killer had started up again in a copycat manner. And while their initial meeting had been rocky, she'd been determined to come to him so they could work together.

Cheyenne knew how to work a case.

But, once again, she was very close to this one. Another cousin was involved.

"French Riviera, I think," he said. "Or maybe Costa del Sol."

"Pardon?"

"When this is solved."

"Andre, we have to work this," she whispered. "We don't have much time. I mean, this needs to be solved, and we aren't British, we're American. And even in the Krewe, we will be expected to return to work—"

"Means we'd better move quickly, right? And, remember, we are human. Meaning we require meals and sleep. Especially if we want our minds to function."

She nodded. "So, back to the house?"

"Back to the house. And put some calls in to Jackson to see what magic Adam can work. And get Angela researching a few of our persons of interest."

Cheyenne smiled and caught Andre's hand. He looked at her. They were always professional on the job.

She laughed. "Hey, we're not official anything here, remember? We're a couple on vacation visiting a relative."

"True." He caught her hand and pulled her against him. Lifting her chin, he kissed her lips. He took a moment to revel in the feel and scent of her.

To his surprise, she pulled away, frowning.

"What?"

She looked around quickly.

They stood on Swain's Lane. A few people moved around them, likely heading home from a day at work. Most either gave them little head nods or smiled at the lovers enjoying one another.

"I felt...I don't know. Like someone was watching us."

"People *are* watching us. We're in a public place."

"Yes, but...uh, sorry."

He stood very still for a minute.

"Monte," he said.

"What?"

"He did follow us into the other side of the cemetery."

"Perhaps his cousin ordered him to spy on us. You don't think—?"

"That he could be a suspect?" Andre asked. "I think anyone could be a suspect. And I think there was something odd about Monte."

"He was nice and knowledgeable," Cheyenne offered. "And curious. Though he did seem to be watching us. But he'd know about us from Inspector Adair."

"Yes."

"So?"

"I don't know. Just...something."

"We'll put him on our list of people to find out more about."

Andre caught her hand again. "Right. So, let's get back, shall we?"

* * * *

Emily had decided that she was going to welcome her family with a large pot of gumbo, cornbread, and boudin—tastes of home.

Cheyenne hugged her cousin and asked Eric how he felt about their homestyle meal.

"Love it when she cooks. She's a marvel. She's taught me all about spices," Eric said.

"He's quite a cook himself," Emily said affectionately.

Eric stood a bit taller. "Which I shall demonstrate tomorrow night."

After they returned from the cemetery, things were very casual. Still, Cheyenne noted that Andre had been doing some texting—back to the States. It would still be day there, and she knew that while they were here unofficially, Angela and Jackson would do whatever they could to help them along from home.

They went about the hustle of getting the meal on the table, and after they all sat down to eat, Cheyenne and Andre told the couple about their day—omitting the part about Lady Elizabeth Miller.

"I've seen pictures on the telly of the most recent woman who went missing," Eric said. "They're saying she was last seen on Swain's Lane. That she left the high-rise to go out with friends, was seen walking back to her family's place, and didn't show up for work this morning. I hate to be pessimistic, but..."

"He's got her," Emily said, her tone sad. "She'll appear somewhere soon enough—her body will, at least. And then the police will be back after us. Why in God's name do they think we're such ghouls?"

"Because they're grasping at straws," Andre told her. "Anytime someone is murdered, police have to look at the spouse or partner first, then the extended family and friends list. Random killings are the hardest to solve. And if this is part of a cult or just an individual with a mental illness, a sociopath or psychopath, finding him or her becomes very difficult. With Sheila, they think they at least have motive. Eric, for your part, you might have been afraid of something she could tell Emily, ruining your relationship. Emily, they may believe that you wanted to get rid of the woman who had opportunity to seize Eric back from you."

"But...that's not true at all!" Emily protested.

"No. Though, as I said, they're grasping. We went to see Father Faith today. He is an interesting character, however...I admit, I didn't get a killer vibe. Although, at the moment, that isn't something I can depend on. We're looking to meet the other persons of interest," Andre assured her.

"Who?" Emily asked anxiously.

"Clark Brighton, Mark Bower, Benjamin Turner. Do any of those names mean anything to you?" Cheyenne asked.

"Of course," Emily said.

"Benjamin Turner has garnered an audience for himself—and a number of sponsors—on his Internet channel," Eric said.

"He does bits on local history, the Tower of London, Whitechapel," Emily added. "And he did a Halloween piece one year about Highgate Cemetery. Many Internet sensations have done that."

"He's local?" Andre asked.

"A bit closer to the heart of London, but local enough," Eric said.

"Have you ever met him?" Cheyenne asked.

Eric nodded. "Why, yes. He also wrote a book. *Bloody Weird History.* He was having a thing at a local bookshop a while back. Can't say I know the chap. Happened in at the end of it all and thought I'd support a somewhat-local author in his endeavor. I bought the book. Met him."

"I wasn't with him," Emily added.

"How did he strike you?" Cheyenne asked Eric.

"Decent. But you can see easily enough for yourself. Just do a search on his name. It will return a few of his videos. They're about five minutes each. He said he was taught that amount of time was pushing the limit of a person's focus these days, but he'd go the five anyway to get in what was important about the subject or place."

"Sheila dated him," Cheyenne said.

"Did she now?" Eric asked.

"But that wasn't something she shared with you," Andre observed.

Eric shrugged. "She owed me no accounting of her dating."

"She also dated a banker. Mark Bower," Cheyenne said.

"Bower, yes. We both know him," Eric told them. "He's with the local branch of our bank. Good fellow, I'd say. A little prim, but a proper British banker. I didn't know that he and Sheila dated. Frankly, he's a bit…well…staid. Then again, who knows what a chap is really like when he's not on the job, eh?"

"Clark Brighton is something of a local celebrity—or nut," Emily said. "He goes on local shows now and then, touting one of his guides or booklets. Let's see… His latest was something called *Let the Moon Beam Down When the Sun Will Not.* I mean, he sounds a bit off his rocker but harmless. Except he rants a lot about the evils of Satan, telling people they always need to look to the light."

Cheyenne caught Andre's eye and knew they were thinking the same thing.

They all sounded like interesting candidates.

Clark Brighton might well be a case of "*the lady doth protest too much, methinks,*" as Shakespeare once said. Except, in this case, it was a man.

Mark Bower, prim and proper by day…something else by night.

Benjamin Turner, a man who knew the past well, with Highgate Cemetery being part of that history.

"Where do we go from here?" Emily asked, her voice a worried whisper with just a touch of a sob.

"We go about life," Andre said firmly. "Cheyenne and I will do our best to meet others in your lineup of interesting characters. Just be careful."

"You think we're in danger?" Eric asked.

"I'd say everyone in this area is in danger until this killer is caught," Andre said. "And, yes. I think you two need to be especially careful. Sheila was an ex-girlfriend. She was found on your steps. I believe the killer knew you had dated and hoped to send the police your way, Eric."

Eric nodded glumly.

Cheyenne suddenly yawned, quickly clamping her hand over her mouth and looking around. "I'm so sorry! It isn't the company."

"Oh, dear," Emily said. "You came all this way, and you've been up for so long. You two should get some sleep. Eric brought your bags up. The guest room is at the top of the stairs to the left. If you need anything at all, just let me know. But you must sleep."

"We will. Though let us help clean up after dinner fi—" Andre started.

"No!" Emily and Eric said in unison, interrupting him.

"Go on upstairs and get to bed. There's a shower in your attached bathroom. I left towels, soap, shampoo—hopefully, anything you might need," Emily said.

"We'll just pick up a few plates—" Cheyenne began.

"No!" Emily protested. "Go!"

"Okay, okay!" Cheyenne paused, drawing her cousin to her for a hug. She tried to reassure her. "We will get to the bottom of this."

"I hope so," Emily said.

"Hey, it's what we do," Andre said, pausing behind Cheyenne. "It's what we do."

Cheyenne turned to him. "Race you up the stairs!" She pushed past him, aware he remained for a minute with Emily.

She heard him say, "I like to let her win now and then. You know?"

"I'll bet she wins plenty on her own." Eric chuckled.

"Yep. She does," Andre agreed. "Goodnight. Windows and doors locked tight, right?"

"Yes, sir, Special Agent Rousseau," Eric said.

A minute later, Cheyenne heard Andre's footsteps as he followed her up the stairs.

She knew it had taken a minute because he was Andre, and he likely checked the windows and the front and back doors himself.

She waited by the bedroom door until he was in the room. Then she slipped her arms around his neck and smiled up at him. "You're a good man. Do you know that?"

"I'm very good. I mean, you know. *Very* good. In many ways," he teased.

"Aw, well, I should be the judge of that, right?" she asked.

"Huh! I'm wounded to the core," he said.

She laughed. "Like hell. It would take far more than a few words from me to wound you to the core."

His dark eyes grew serious. "No, my love, you are the only one with the ability to wound me to the core." He kissed her lips. A long kiss that started gently, becoming deeper and more passionate. She felt the pressure of his body against hers—along with the growth of his desire—and stepped back.

"Race you into the shower!" she said.

"No! Are you kidding? I shall take my time to join you, rather than have one of us slip on some unseen bit of soap, crash to the floor, break a bone, and totally ruin the moment."

She laughed and turned for the bathroom in the guest room, shedding her clothing as she walked in.

He was very close behind her.

They needed a decent shower. They'd been on a plane for hours, and then they'd spent a large portion of the day in a cemetery.

But...

Soaping up became far more than a bid for cleanliness.

Rinsing, not so important.

Using the fluffy towels to dry was more of a promise than a real fight against moisture, and they were quickly entangled with one another and falling onto the bed. The washing had been great, though, and Cheyenne loved the feel of Andre's skin as she ran her lips and fingers across him, luxuriating as he touched her in turn. He had an amazing ability to tease and build desire within her, to please and withdraw, and then give so fully that she felt as if the world itself might burst into a rain of firelit pleasure. Within her at last, he paused a moment and whispered, "Making love— first time in England." He grinned. "Diary notation," he teased.

She laughed and pulled him back to her, urging him into a deep, long kiss that escalated with his movements inside her. Thrust and parry…the fireworks coming ever closer.

After, they lay together, his arms around her. She knew his thoughts had gone back to the matter at hand.

They had both learned that while the job might rule their world most days, there were also times that, no matter how dire, they had to be together. They took the moments they stole to remember the beauty of life when set against all they had witnessed.

But now…

"We know there's something going on. I can't get over being in the catacombs…or mausoleum—whatever one officially calls the places we visited—because it showed how clearly there can be confined spaces in the ground and above the ground."

"Elizabeth said the earth was moaning," Cheyenne said. "I think it's obvious. The killer is taking his victims underground somewhere. Elizabeth said it came from the high point of the lane. There could be dozens of subterranean tunnels. I mean, I read online that there is a tunnel that connects the cemetery's east and west sides."

"You think the person is killing his victims *in* the cemetery?" Andre asked thoughtfully. "I mean, it's possible. Despite walls and gates and the determination against vandalism and so on that began in the mid-seventies, people who want in will find a way. But I don't think our killer would be so obvious. Highgate is convenient. The story about the Vampire of Highgate is convenient, too. I believe you're right. But I don't think we'll get much support if we start digging up the streets."

"The killer didn't just dig up the streets," she said.

"No. But with this topography, all manner of things could have been constructed at any time throughout the hundreds of years of history. There might have been natural caverns, covered over now. Time does a number on things."

"Ah. Suggests a historian?" Cheyenne murmured.

"We need to meet the rest of these characters tomorrow. And guess who else we need to meet?"

"Who?"

"Birmingham."

"Why? He wants nothing to do with us."

"Yes, and that bothers me. He's very cold and dismissive."

"Some people are like that. We all know most cops and agents are certainly decent when working together, and there aren't nearly as many jurisdictional creeps as some people think, but we are Americans. In Britain."

"Right. Still."

"Yes?"

"He's a jerk."

Cheyenne laughed and rose against him, straddling him.

"Ah, sir, you have a wicked tongue!"

"I speak only truth."

"I wasn't referring to speech," she told him solemnly. "And, in truth, I am quite fond of your very, very wicked tongue."

His dark eyes narrowed upon her with laughter, and he teased her with a Scottish brogue. "Ah, lass! I'll show you a wicked tongue, I will!"

"Promises, promises!" she giggled, but then they were kissing again and then escalating and making love and…

He did prove he had a deliciously and wondrously wicked tongue.

Chapter 6

"You have information on all of them?" Andre asked. He'd stepped outside when his phone rang. It was early morning here, so he knew it was late in D.C. for Angela.

"Quite a bit, actually. I'll email it all and start with the banker, Mark Bower," she said.

"Still waters running deep?"

"Maybe. He goes to work every day and, in the past, has had a tendency to date women much like him—serious nine-to-fivers. But we've also discovered several pictures of him that came out recently on social media. In them, he's attending a club that sounds like it's a bit on the wild side. A strip club. He enjoys a lot of, shall we say, *expensive* female companionship. That does make him interesting, though it is a leap to go from strip clubs and prostitutes to draining the blood out of murder victims."

"Agreed. What else?"

"No arrest record, not even parking tickets. Until recently, he's been a Boy Scout."

"Okay. Benjamin Turner?"

"I need more hours than you and I have together. He started his own media channel about five years ago. Since then, he's been everywhere. He does have a penchant for bringing the weird to life. He's done the necessary bit on Jack the Ripper, a segment on H.H. Holmes, Madam Bathory, Vlad the Impaler, the Yorkshire Ripper, Burke and Hare...and so on. Naturally, he's done Highgate. Check out the video yourself. He was born in north London, a few miles from where he lives today. He definitely has a penchant for creepy people and things, but so do many, many others. He's handsome and charismatic."

"I'm thinking our killer is handsome and charismatic. He's luring his victims somehow," Andre said.

"Yes, well, then I have the last name on your list. And I also checked out the other fellow you mentioned, William Smith, Father Faith."

"And?"

"Clark Brighton. Claims he's a bishop in the Church of the Shining Spiritualists, but I checked data sources from just about everywhere."

"And there is no Church of the Shining Spiritualists."

"Right. But he seems to be benign, spouting cheer and optimism, seeking wisdom from rainbows, that kind of thing. And he does have a following. Seems he may not have a church himself, but he knows a lot about Satanism and is continually damning them. Oh! And have you seen him?"

"Not yet."

"You'd be expecting a wizened, creepy little man. Maybe. I was. But, no. He looks like a California beach boy. Tall, blond, middle-aged, good-looking. He finds happiness rowing and at the gym."

"Strong?"

"I would imagine. But none of your guys is too small to subdue a woman. Not that you need size. He's probably luring them and knocking them out or doing something to make them more pliable. I have the medical examiner's reports on the women who were killed, and there is nothing in their toxicology. All of them had alcohol in their systems, but none to the point of drunkenness. They would have been aware—unless they were made somehow *un*aware. Some substances aren't tested for in general autopsies, or if the cause of death is evident—such as having the blood drained from the body. So, it's unlikely a medical examiner would have searched for them. Remember, many things are possible, but most government facilities tend to be short on funds and use their budgets judiciously."

"Right."

"On to Father Faith," Angela said.

"Yes, please. And thanks."

"He might be a Brit, but he's a pure capitalist," she said. "Apparently, he was asked to be a vampire in a B movie about fifteen years ago—he had the look—and discovered it brought him all kinds of fame. He turned that into being a psychic, learning about tarot cards, tea leaves, and all manner of fortune-telling and divination. He had two shops for a while, one near the Tower of London, and the one in Highgate. Highgate brought in a massive clientele. He carries books written by all those associated with the Highgate vampire craze and more. I get the impression that he's all for show."

"Him, I did meet. And I agree. But that doesn't mean he isn't living a secret life."

"Well, that's what I have so far. If you need specifics or more on different suspects, we're here for you."

"I know that, and thank you again."

"How is Cheyenne doing?"

"She's okay."

"Another cousin after...well, losing a cousin all those years ago. Do you think Emily is in danger?"

"I'm still trying to figure out what I think," Andre said. "And I am trying to rush that along. We're down to four days before Halloween. And—"

"Yes, Halloween is already crazy here! We've had to send agents out on Halloween-related cases, as well. I didn't think the Brits embraced the holiday the way we do, though."

"They don't go all in, but it's becoming more popular. But this isn't most of Britain. This is Highgate. Where some still believe in vampires, vampire hunters, vampire kids...and a killer is stealing blood and life. So...I guess that *is* a vampire, too."

"By sick definition, yes. Okay. So, give Cheyenne our best, and call or text if you need anything. And, Andre," she said seriously, "be careful."

"Always."

"Extra careful."

"Yes, ma'am."

"Adam is working on a diplomatic angle to get you more access. I'll be back in touch when I have something on that."

"Sounds good."

As he ended the call, he found himself looking at the front steps.

Someone had scrawled letters on the lower one.

He stooped low to read them and then groaned aloud.

Two words had been written in chalk.

Blood Night.

"What the hell does that mean?" he muttered aloud.

As he did so, the front door opened, and Cheyenne stepped out, frowning as she saw him crouched down, staring at the porch step and muttering.

He shook his head, and she came down the steps to join him.

"Blood Night?" she read aloud, looking at him. "What the hell?"

"We have to call Inspector Adair on this," Andre said to her.

"I believe it was the title of a movie." She shook her head. "I don't know if it's in reference to a rite, but I don't know about all of that. And, as we know, anyone can make up their own church these days. But maybe it's just a taunt. Someone who wants to make Emily and Eric look bad," Cheyenne added hopefully.

Andre was already dialing Adair.

Emily came to the door, smiling. "Hey, guys, breakfast! Eric wanted to start early. He whipped up one of his fantastic major-league English breakfasts. So much stuff…"

Her voice trailed off.

"Oh, God, what is it?" she asked.

"A prankster, probably," Cheyenne said lightly.

Emily ran outside. She, too, hunkered down.

"Hey, Yankee bloke and lady!" Eric called playfully from the doorway. "Breakfast—"

He fell silent and then walked out to join the others, stooping down, as well.

Eric phrased his question differently.

"What the *bloody hell* is that supposed to mean?" he demanded angrily.

Andre finally reached Inspector Adair and asked him to come out. When he was finished with the call, he used his phone to take pictures of the writing on the step.

The others looked at him.

"Breakfast," he said. "Go on in. I'll join you as soon as Adair comes. I don't want to take the chance of anyone erasing this before the inspector sees it."

They all kept staring at him.

"I am excited about Eric's cooking," he assured them. "I'll just be a few minutes."

Emily and Eric kept staring. Their faces pale, stunned, and he thought, scared.

"Hey, Andre's got it," Cheyenne finally said firmly, shooing them toward the door. "Let's go in. You're not providing just pastries and juice.

I love a full English breakfast!"

Neither Emily nor Eric responded, but they let Cheyenne usher them back into the house.

Andre took a seat on the porch far enough away from the writing so he didn't mar or brush it with his legs.

And he waited, curious what Inspector Adair would think the message meant.

* * * *

"It's a fry-up over here, mostly because almost everything is fried. Well, not the fruit and juice," Eric said, obviously babbling somewhat, determined to take Emily's mind off the writing on their step. He looked at Cheyenne. "So, voilà! You will see we have bangers—sausages to you, I believe, though I know you're familiar with the term—and bacon, fried eggs, fried tomatoes, and even the mushrooms are fried. Whoops, I didn't fry the bread. That's straight out of the toaster."

"It all looks great. Right, Emily?" Cheyenne said.

Emily forced a plastic smile. "Lovely."

"Shall we?" Cheyenne motioned to the food, glad she was hungry. Because she, too, wanted to know what the hell the writing on the step meant.

She sat, looking up and waiting for her cousin and Eric, surely showing them that she couldn't possibly begin to eat unless they joined her.

They sat, and Eric picked up his fork.

Cheyenne grabbed her utensils and dug in, starting with the tomato and eggs.

"Wonderful!"

Both her cousin and Eric stared at her, so she set down her flatware. "Oh, please. Come on. That could have been a prank by a teenager. It could mean nothing at all."

"You don't believe that," Emily said. "I don't know all about your criminology college courses or what you do with the Krewe of Hunters, but I know you all have some kind of gut instincts. You don't believe that."

"Everyone has gut instincts," Cheyenne said. "Okay, I don't know what is going on yet. But we'll be here until we figure it out. Okay? And I know you two aren't guilty of anything. We'll get through all this."

"You know Emily," Eric said bleakly. "You don't know me all that well, Cheyenne. What if I'm a crazed killer and I don't even know it?" He paused, turning to Emily. "Oh, God, Emily!"

"Eric, you're not a crazed killer," Emily said. She stood and walked around to him, placing her arms around his shoulders and hugging him for a minute. "That you'd even think that way—that's crazy. And you don't believe it."

He held her in return. "No," he said softly. "I don't. I just wanted to give you an out if you wanted one."

"Well, I don't. And I didn't kill your ex-girlfriend either," Emily said with certainty. She managed a real smile then. "If we were crazed killers, we'd have to have a different method of murder. Eric and I don't even like to help each other with a scratch."

"Not blood people," Eric agreed weakly.

"Okay, I'm glad that's settled. And this breakfast is delicious. I'm going to get back to it, and you two need to eat up. Andre will be back in any minute. He's going to love this."

Andre returned a few minutes later. Cheyenne had finished eating, and she hopped up, looking at him expectantly but instead asking, "Would you like your breakfast warmed up? It might be a little cold now."

"Naw, I work for the federal government. I've come to like cold food," he said lightly and sat at the place setting where his food waited. But he didn't eat. He smiled, aware that they were all waiting.

"Inspector Adair came and photographed the steps and duly noted the bit of minor vandalism. He'll include it in his files. He's gone now."

"He could have come in for breakfast," Eric said.

Andre shrugged. "No, he's on the case. Breaking bread with us wouldn't be a wise thing for him at the moment." He shifted his attention to the food. "Wow. This looks great, Eric, thank you," he said and started to eat.

"Pleasure," Eric murmured.

Andre swallowed and took a sip of juice. "I also sent some pics I took to Krewe headquarters. We'll see if anything comes up. In the meantime, Cheyenne and I are going to head out to meet a few people and see what we can find. I suggest you two try to relax here. Keep close to home. What about work?" he asked.

"I'm good from home," Eric said.

Emily nodded. "I asked for leave. I didn't say it was because the police think I'm a deranged killer. I just told them family was coming in from the States."

"Great," Andre said.

"How do we relax?" Emily wondered, not really addressing any of them.

"Movies!" Eric said. "We can cook and clean and watch movies."

Andre had finished his plate of food in the few minutes they'd been talking. He stood up, placing his napkin by his dish.

"Movies, cleaning, whatever. Sit tight this morning. Maybe we'll go out together tonight, mingle with the community, see if anyone notices. Or we'll see if there's anything unusual when we get back. I've also asked Inspector Adair to see if he can make sure the regular patrolmen keep an eye on your home. Did you know there is surprisingly little CCTV coverage of any kind in this area?" He hesitated. "Hey, that's it. Security cameras. I'm going to see that you have a few installed today. How about it?"

"Oh, I don't..." Emily said and paused. "I'm not sure we can afford a system like that right now."

"Housewarming gift." Cheyenne smiled.

"Cheyenne, I've been living here for over a year, and it's been Eric's home since he bought it from his folks a decade ago," Emily said.

"Wow, I'm late with that gift!" Cheyenne said. "So, we're going to let you two pick up alone again. Sorry. But we're out of here. And don't you dare refuse to accept a gift from me. Andre...Andre knows people. We'll get the best for the buck. Um, *pound*. And with your computer skills, you'll know what to do with it, Eric," she promised.

"Andre knows people in Highgate?" Emily asked.

"He gets around," Cheyenne said.

She didn't let Emily argue, just glanced at Andre, who murmured another, "Thanks for breakfast, Eric, it was great!"

Then he quickly followed her out of the house.

Chapter 7

"So, I know people in Highgate now, do I?" Andre asked, smiling.

"You seem to know everyone you meet right away," Cheyenne said. "Seriously, Andre, if they'd had a security camera outside, they could have seen who did this."

"We should have woken up. *I* should have woken up," he said.

"Andre, you're human, and so am I. When we slept, we slept hard last night."

He didn't argue that. He looked ahead. Cheyenne had just started walking—without a plan, without knowing where she was going. But he strolled right along with her.

She stopped. "Uh, where are we going?"

"We're starting with a visit to Clark Brighton."

She glanced at him. They were walking uphill toward the new, luxury apartments.

"We have an appointment with him, and you know he's there?" she asked.

"We don't have an appointment, but I know he's there. I talked to Michael Adair about him when the good inspector came to see the writing on the steps. Mr. Brighton spends his mornings down at a coffee shop on the ground floor of his building. He likes to hold court there."

"Do you think Inspector Adair's partner, Birmingham, informed him that we're with the American government? Feds?"

He smiled. "Yep, I think he did."

"Then this guy won't see us—"

"He will." Andre glanced her way. "Adair thought it was funny as all hell. Birmingham wanted to warn his suspects away from talking to us. He told Brighton we were psyched-up ghost hunters. I guess he didn't realize that would make the man want to see us all the more. I think he'll be happy to talk to us."

"If he's happy to talk to us, he's either innocent or truly a flake," she said.

"We'll find out. Hey, isn't there a saying? '*Out of the mouths of flakes?*'"

"No, it's '*out of the mouths of babes,*' but you know that, of course."

"I could have sworn it was out of the mouths of flakes!" he teased. "Come on. We have to meet all the persons of interest we know about and then try to see if we've been going in the right direction. I texted Angela, who told me to let them know if we needed anything. I've got her checking out the lives, social media, and habits of the other victims. Right now, the concentration is on Sheila. Probably because her landing on an ex-boyfriend's steps seemed awfully convenient."

"We have to get them cameras and a system today."

"We will. There's an electronics shop up here, too. We're good. I must admit, I don't know people there, but I'm sure I will."

Cheyenne wasn't sure just how luxurious the *luxury* apartments were, but they were new. Looking up, she saw they offered amazing rooftop patios with views of the lower area of town, the steep slope down Swain's Lane, and Highgate Cemetery. The place seemed to be made up of a lot of angles, glass, and chrome. It was plain but almost squeaky clean, and the coffee shop on the ground floor was ultra-modern and encased mostly in glass, which allowed them to see Clark Brighton easily before they entered. He was seated so they couldn't see his height. But his shoulders were broad and strong, and his hair was only lightly peppered with gray.

"Coffee, my love? Or tea?" Andre asked.

"Coffee. I'll go over with an introduction," Cheyenne said.

Andre walked up to the counter to order, and Cheyenne headed toward the man who hadn't yet noticed her. He was concentrating intently on whatever he was reading on his computer.

He looked up as he heard her coming, though. There was a confused look in his eyes at first, but then he smiled broadly, rising to offer her a hand.

He was tall. Not quite as tall as Andre, but almost. A big man. A strong man.

"You're the American from the Krewe of Hunters, right?" he asked her.

"Just Cheyenne Donegal over here, Mr. Brighton. Truly grateful to make your acquaintance," she said, shaking his hand. "May I?" She indicated the chairs on the other side of the table from him. "Or may *we*. Andre Rousseau is with me. We're eager to hear what you have to say. I mean, something awful is happening. Something out of the ordinary."

"Someone who intends to listen to me," Brighton said. "Yes, yes. Please. I keep trying to tell the police that ignoring the past is dangerous."

"We all know ignoring the past is dangerous," Cheyenne agreed. "And we've been doing all we can to steep ourselves in the history of what happened here before. Do you think someone has really summoned a...vampire?" she asked.

He nodded. "Though a vampire can mean many things. Our greatest threat is those who would meddle in such awful creatures."

"Satanists?"

"Yes, well, freedom of religion these days, you know. But who was Satan? Cast from heaven—the harbinger of evil and...can a person be a Satanist and not be evil? How is that, by the very nature of the devil's existence, possible? I've told them, I've told the police that the very earth is crying." The expression on Clark Brighton's face said that he was serious.

"What?"

"Several times now, and right before one of the kidnapped girls is found, dead and drained of blood. The earth itself cries. As if calling out to all that's good and holy in the world to help."

Andre walked over, bearing three cups of coffee and a paper sack brimming with creamers and sugar.

He quickly set them down and offered Clark Brighton a hand. "Andre Rousseau—"

"Don't be so modest. You're Special Agent Andre Rousseau with the FBI's legendary Krewe of Hunters," Clark said, rising to take Andre's hand. "And this unbelievably lovely young lady is Special Agent Cheyenne Donegal. I am glad to make your acquaintance, truly glad. I've just begun speaking with Cheyenne here."

"He was telling me that he heard the earth cry," Cheyenne supplied.

Andre arched a brow. "The earth, sir?"

"I was trying to tell the law officers that they're not doing their duty. I truly fear Satanists are taking a secret stand here."

"Do you believe they've caused a vampire to rise?" Andre asked seriously.

"I say again, as I did to your lovely partner earlier, define *vampire!*" Brighton looked as if he wanted to pound the table in his vehemence. "What I believe is that they are seeking blood. They must have it! *They* are the vampires themselves!"

"Sir, wouldn't they have been noticed? It would be difficult these days for them to use the cemetery as a site for rituals, wouldn't it?"

Clark Brighton waved a hand in the air. "Have you ever noticed, sir, criminals don't obey our laws? That's what makes them criminals. Trust me. There are ways into the cemetery at night. There is always a way, especially with an area that large. But I don't know if they're using the cemetery. They are here, though. I sense things, hear things in the air. In the night. I am a special person, as you two are special people, and I have senses others do not. I tell you, the earth itself is crying. And it lets out moans and wails, right before another of the victims is found. You will look into this, won't you?" He leaned forward to gaze intensely at them.

"We're not here officially," Cheyenne reminded him.

Clark stared at her hard and slowly smiled. "But you're here."

"We will listen for when the earth cries, sir," Andre assured him. He hesitated. "Is there anything else you can tell us?"

Brighton shook his head, his expression sad. "I wish I saw more, but all my vision has allowed me so far is misty shapes. The warning came with those cries from the very ground we walk upon, from the air, and from the night. It's only when all else is silent that you can hear them." He was quiet for a minute. "Late, late at night, I've stood out on my balcony, and I have heard the earth. I promised I would listen."

"Mr. Brighton, you may rest assured that we, too, will listen," Andre said earnestly. "I promise you."

He rose then, and Cheyenne followed.

"Thank you so much."

"No. Thank you," Brighton told her. "And, you," he said to Andre.

Andre nodded grimly. He set a hand on Cheyenne's arm, and they walked out together.

"Flake, but I believe you were right. Out of the mouths of flakes."

"Well, we've heard it now from the living *and* the dead. The earth is crying."

"Think Inspector Adair will believe us?" Cheyenne asked.

"I think we need maps, old and new, but I also believe we're looking at the high end of the lane. Possibly someone digging when the cemetery was planned. We might be looking for a basement, but I don't think so. I believe there is a subterranean catacomb, storage space, original throughway—*something* underground that the killer is using for a lair. There's no way he's puncturing throats and taking the time to bleed someone where he could be seen or caught."

"We need to talk to the inspector."

"Adair and Birmingham both. Hopefully, Adam has gotten through to someone who knows someone who will help us."

"And now?"

"I think we need to exchange more money."

"Ah, you take this one. I think it will be a bit more natural if you ask the banker about the strip clubs he visits."

He grinned. "How many times do you think people walk into banks and ask about strip clubs?"

"Not every day?"

"Trust me, this dude is going to know we're coming. We'll find out if he'll talk to us or not. We really do need to meet Inspector Birmingham."

"I agree. Are we about to change more dollars into pounds?"

"We are. Just down the lane."

But as he spoke, Andre stopped walking. Instead, he looked up Swain's Lane.

"They used to drive the swine down this way to the market at Spitalfields," he said. "Thus, Swain's Lane."

"And cliffs and rises aplenty all around."

"And Highgate, overgrown—much like home. Decaying elegance, haunting atmosphere—well, we've had a Rougarou. Might as well have a vampire," he said.

"And our *flake* was right about something else," Cheyenne said.

"Yeah?"

"Define vampire. This killer is abducting women and draining them of blood. That would be a vampire by definition. Hey, let's get the car later and just drive all the way up and explore the heights, huh?"

"Sure. Bank, electronics shop, and drive. But what about our last man?"

"Internet sensation Benjamin Turner?"

"That would be him. We'll get to him, too," Andre promised. "You got money?"

"Some. I mostly have pounds right now."

"Me, too. Oh, well. I'll switch some back." He chuckled.

They reached the bank. Andre went in ahead, and she followed a minute later.

It didn't matter.

While she pretended to be studying a rack of pamphlets advertising credit cards, Andre strode in as if he were looking for where he should be going for currency exchange.

A man rose from the desk on the side of the bank and walked out of a little gated-off section, making his apologies to the older woman who was sitting in front of his desk.

He headed straight for Andre and kept his voice low, but Cheyenne could hear him.

"I know who you are, and I do not wish to speak with you. The police have questioned me. I hadn't seen Sheila in weeks. I don't care if one of your American oh-so-special agents is Emily Donegal's cousin. You have no authority here, and don't you dare think you're going to question me at my place of business."

Andre just stared at him for a moment as if puzzled. "Oh, you must be that banker. Mark Bower, right?"

"Yes. Will you please be so kind as to leave now before I'm forced to call security?"

"I just need to exchange some coins. I've accumulated a stack of them already."

Cheyenne decided it was time for her entry. She left the rack of pamphlets and approached the two of them. "Andre, we need to get going. I'm sorry, sir!" she said to Mark Bower. "We just need to get rid of some of these coins. I mean, they'll be worthless when we get home, and you kind of wind up with them no matter how hard you try to get rid of them."

"You're just here to exchange money?" Bower asked.

"We are."

"But—"

"Well, you and Sheila weren't close, were you? I mean, you only dated a few times, right?"

"Right. We dated a few times," Bower said. "That's it. I'm sorry. She was a nice girl. But I am not talking to any *unauthorized* Americans about the case. I will thank you to get out of the bank."

"May we just exchange our coins for paper currency, please?" Cheyenne asked sweetly.

Bower leaned back slightly, crossing his arms over his chest. "You just happened into this bank, right?"

"Well, old chap," Andre said, "it's the first bank we came to on the street. Apparently, you know about us. So, you likely know we're staying with Eric and Emily because you know Sheila was found on their doorstep. This is the nearest bank," Andre pointed out.

"Do your business and get out," Bower snapped.

Andre politely told him, "Thank you," and headed for the counter.

"Why are you so against us?" Cheyenne asked.

She was surprised at the sudden passion Bower showed when he turned to her. "Sheila is dead. And we don't need any seances or any other mumbo-jumbo used against her memory. She's dead. Do you get that? Dead!"

He spun around and headed back to his desk and his customer, adjusting his tie as he did, apologizing profusely to the older woman who awaited him.

"The electronics store is just a bit down," Andre said, returning with a small stack of colorful British pounds in his hand. "First things first. Cameras and cables. And then—"

He didn't finish his sentence because his phone started ringing.

He answered it quickly. By the way his expression changed, she knew it had to be the home office calling.

He listened, nodded, glanced at his watch, and took Cheyenne gently by the arm to lead her outside.

Back on the street, he stopped, agreed to whatever was being said on the other end of the line, and then ended the call before looking at her.

"So?" Cheyenne asked.

"Well, I was going to say we needed a trip to meet with the esteemed Inspector Birmingham, but that will have to wait. If we move swiftly, we have a few minutes to get a camera set up—at least something—for Eric and Emily's place."

"Yes, I think that may prove to be really important."

"I want to meet Birmingham, though." He grimaced. "I'm tempted to tell him I've received a message from his long-lost dog or something—that it came through my crystal ball."

"Andre! We need to be careful here. I don't think mocking Bower by calling him a *chap* was...diplomatic."

"Hey, I love the British. And even I love the sound of a smooth accent. He just came on like such an ass. I'm sorry. And you're right."

"Remember—"

"Yes, we're not official. Anyway, we'll meet Birmingham eventually, but Angela also gave me the name of the club Bower visits most frequently. It's called Pussycats and Toms, and it's down at Piccadilly Circus. We'll go tonight."

"Great. I love a good strip club." She rolled her eyes.

He grinned, arched a brow, and moved again toward the electronics store.

"It is called Pussycats and Toms. Maybe there are some good Toms to be seen."

"I think the *Toms* part probably refers to the customers, but I'm up for whatever. You think Bower is worth the time?"

"I do."

"All right, but why not Birmingham now? We can buy our cameras and all, drop them off at Eric and Emily's, and we'll still be early. It's just after ten."

"We have an appointment."

"With?"

"Benjamin Turner, historian and Internet sensation."

Chapter 8

Andre could easily see why Benjamin Turner had managed to become an Internet sensation.

He was a tall man, fit, with bright blue eyes and reddish-brown hair, a quick smile, and a way of looking very serious and intelligent.

When they arrived—after their visit to the electronics store and their stop by the house to deliver their purchases to Eric, who was delighted to play with the equipment and his computer through the afternoon—a man met them and asked them to wait behind the glass of a home studio.

The assistant wasn't doing the filming. He'd been sitting at his desk when they arrived, obviously taking care of some mundane things. Perhaps like accounting or the research needed for many of Turner's little broadcasts.

Turner had his studio set up so he managed his own cameras. Andre assumed he did his own editing, as well.

He was currently working on a leading-up-to-Halloween broadcast, revisiting gory events around the world that had occurred right before the holiday.

The most recent one was a piece on the toolbox killers who had tortured and killed five women, with the last murder taking place in the United States on Halloween, 1979.

He went into gory detail, cinematically somber, warning his watchers to be safe. Every year, there were more parties in Britain with Halloween becoming more of an event resembling that of the States.

Turner finished with the broadcast and turned off the camera and microphones he had in the studio.

Then he looked through the glass and smiled at them.

Exiting his recording space, he introduced himself, in case they hadn't been aware of who they were watching.

"Hello, welcome. I'm Benjamin Turner. I talked to an absolutely lovely young American woman a few hours ago, who asked if I would speak with you. I'm happy to do so! I don't know how I can be of assistance, but if there's anything I can say or do that might help, I am delighted."

Andre introduced himself and then Cheyenne, and then jumped right into the reason for their visit. "We understand that you knew the last victim, Sheila Lynsey," he stated.

Turner's face took on a pained and dark look. "Sheila was…well, we were casual, but we might have been more. I'll never know now. I was devastated to hear…what happened to her."

"I imagine you'll be doing a show on this in the future," Cheyenne said.

Benjamin shook his head. "Too close," he said softly. "So, tea, coffee, soft drinks, water? May I get you anything?"

"No, no, we're fine, thank you."

"Then please have a seat here in the green room—my parlor—and we'll talk."

He led them to their seats on the sofa. He chose an armchair facing them, his hands folded before him as he leaned toward them anxiously. "I know about you. You're good," he told them, nodding gravely.

"Through Special Agent Angela Hawkins? She made this appointment for us," Andre said.

"Oh, I knew about you before that. I follow cases, you know. I was thrilled when she said members of the Krewe of Hunters wanted to see me. Well, I mean, I wasn't happy about the circumstances, but…I'm honored to meet you."

"That's very kind," Cheyenne said. "What more can you tell us about Sheila? Do you have any idea who she might have met? Any clue whatsoever as to what might have happened to her between visiting two elderly women and winding up, drained of blood, on a doorstep?"

"The banker," he said softly.

"Mark Bower?" Andre asked.

Cheyenne gave him a warning look. Nope, he hadn't liked Bower one bit. But he was aware that, sometimes, the nicest person could prove to be a killer while a jerk was…just a jerk.

"She stopped seeing him, you know. She said when she met him that he was a nice man, polite, caring, concerned. But she was never head-over-heels in love with him. She said things suddenly changed after they'd been going out for a bit," Turner told them.

"Changed how?" Cheyenne asked.

"He…he wanted her to do things."

"Like what?" Andre prompted.

Turner looked uncomfortable and fidgeted a bit before sighing. "He wanted her to dress up like a French maid. No big deal, I suppose. I have a friend who has a wife who likes him to dress like the pool man. He does, and they have great sex. Sorry, I mean…so, the French maid bit wasn't anything too weird, but then he wanted to tie her up and pretend to be a rapist."

"And that didn't work for Sheila?"

He shook his head. "It took me the longest time to get her to talk about…what went on. And it only started because we ran into Mark Bower when we were out at an Italian restaurant one night. We were waiting for a table when he walked in. I believe he had a date with him, but the young lady never made it through the door. He burst in and headed for the hostess like he was the king of the world or some such thing, and then he saw Sheila. He turned and almost knocked her over in his haste to get out. I was about to accost him, I mean, not start a fistfight or anything, just tell him he was rude. But Sheila begged me to just let him go. She told me they'd had a bad break-up, and then over pasta parmigiana, she told me things had gotten more than weird. In truth, she didn't use the word *weird*. She was too sweet for that. She said he was into practices that didn't appeal to her. That made me happy. I'm a straight shooter, and I don't need any props to be pleased, and I sure as hell don't need them to please someone else." He stopped speaking as if realizing that his words sounded almost like an endorsement for his virility.

He turned a dark shade of red and quickly added, "Oh, wow. That was awful. I just meant…Well, forgive me, I'm not judging or anything, I just meant that I…that Bower's way is not…not, oh, man, please, like I said, I'm not judging. Whatever it is, if you have consenting adults, it's cool. It's just that Sheila didn't want to be a consenting adult in…and…wow, sorry!"

He broke off, looking awkwardly at Cheyenne. Andre lowered his head, smiling. Turner needn't have worried. Long before she had so recently become part of the Krewe, Cheyenne Donegal had been an agent. One who studied criminology and crime in all its guises. She'd pretty much seen and heard it all.

"It's okay," she told Turner, and Andre knew she was slightly amused by Turner's declaration regarding his own sexuality. "Really, it's okay. I've heard far worse, and I understand what you're trying to tell us."

"Uh, yes. Thank you."

"Did you tell the detectives on the case about this?" Cheyenne asked.

"I did."

"And?" Andre asked.

"Apparently, Mark Bower had an alibi for the night Sheila disappeared." He stopped speaking and frowned. "Weird."

"What?" Cheyenne asked.

Turner stood suddenly, going for a notebook that lay open on a coffee table across the room by his entertainment center.

"Weird," he repeated.

"So you said. How so?" Cheyenne asked.

"Well, Sheila was taken…she left her friends' place at the new apartments at about nine at night. And she was found on the doorstep at about seven the following morning."

"Right," Andre said, studying their host. "I know what you're probably wondering about. The other victims were reported missing several days before their bodies were found."

"Exactly. But Sheila disappeared at night, and was found the following morning," Turner said. He looked at them. "Does that mean anything?"

"It might," Andre said.

Turner stared at him as if he didn't want to hear someone echo his own thought. "Two killers? Draining bodies of blood?"

"Maybe, but unlikely. Sheila, like the other two women, was found drained of blood, with no pools or even droplets of it anywhere near her. The killer is holding his victims somewhere," Andre said, and then hesitated before adding, "torturing them emotionally through fear, at the very least, before draining them of their blood. In every case, from the crime scene reports and medical examiner statements we've been able to read, it seems they are quickly exsanguinated once the process begins. The puncture wounds, made to appear like the fanged bite of a vampire, are directly in the carotid, and…" He hesitated again. For all the creepy gore Benjamin Turner made use of in his Internet show, he was looking a little nauseous.

The red that had filled his face after his sex talk was now gone, replaced by a pasty white color.

"I believe he's hanging them up like animals in a slaughterhouse, draining the blood that way," Andre said. "I'm sorry."

Turner sat again, his notebook still in his hand. "They haven't said," he told them glumly. "Were they...sexually assaulted?"

"No," Andre told him.

Benjamin Turner looked away for a moment. "Well, I don't know what that means. I still think that prim and proper banker, Mark Bower, the one who turns kinky and becomes a weirdo by the light of the full moon, might be your man. I just hope—"

"Yes?" Cheyenne asked softly.

"There's another girl missing. I hope that..."

"So do we," Andre said, rising. Cheyenne came to her feet, as well, thanking Turner for his time.

"Mr. Turner, may we call on you again?" Cheyenne rummaged in her purse. "We'll give you our numbers. Feel free to call either of us."

She offered him her card, and Andre did the same.

"I'm going to put these right into my speed-dial," Benjamin Turner assured them. "And, thank you. I will. Please, I don't know what else I could say or do, but...call me anytime."

"We'll do that," Andre promised, and they left at last.

* * * *

Andre put through another call to their home office when they left. When he finished, he was frowning.

"You don't mind me doing the talking to the home office, do you?"

She smiled at him. "Andre, we've both been FBI. But I'm brand new to the Krewe of Hunters. Yes, I am fine with you doing the talking. Anything?"

"Well, let's see. We have the cops thinking Eric wanted to get rid of Sheila. But in the meantime, we have this lovely Inspector Birmingham running around telling people that they shouldn't be talking to us. Luckily, two of those people have their own agendas and talked to us anyway. Then, there could still be a random killer not on anyone's radar out there. I don't like Mark Bower. I do like both our Benjamin Turner and Clark Brighton—even if Brighton is a little bit flaky. Doesn't mean a damned thing, as we've said. We need to get information on the other victims, see if anything matches up. And I want to meet Inspector Birmingham."

"I meant from Angela. Did you get anything from Angela?" Cheyenne asked him.

"Just that she tried to reach Birmingham for me. And he's conveniently out of the office today, which Angela should understand since he has a lot to investigate."

"You're just angry that he wants to solve the case himself."

"I don't want to solve the damned thing for him. I want to help so it *can* be solved," Andre said. He glanced at his watch again. "Let's head in. I'd like to see the street, the strip club, and everything else before we head in to watch for action tonight. It's also getting late, and that coffee we had, and even Eric's English breakfast is fading…food would be good."

"I'm going to check in with Emily. Make sure they have their cameras up and running. I'm worried about them, Andre."

"If they lock up and stay vigilant, they'll be fine."

Cheyenne thought about their house on the high end of Swain's Lane. Near the ultra-modern apartments and businesses but close to Highgate Cemetery, too. By night, that area was dark. And on either side of the lane, the trees and foliage grew lushly, shadows reigned, and the tombs of the dead could hide many a sin.

Andre was heading to the car, focused and determined.

She smiled and followed, calling her cousin as she slid into the passenger seat and buckled her belt.

Emily was fine.

Eric was thrilled with the cameras and system they had bought. He was happily playing with his computer and making sure all angles of the house were covered.

"Everything okay?" Andre asked her when she ended the call.

"Yep. They're good. So, driving here is okay, huh?" she asked.

He cast her a glance and smiled. "Still don't trust me on this side of the road?"

"No, I always trust you."

His smile deepened, but he kept his eyes on the road.

"And I trust you. With everything. I was going to say 'my life,' but you *are* my life, you know."

She laughed. "There you go with that wicked tongue again."

"Sorry, I'm driving, or I'd show you."

"Ha, ha." She was silent for a minute. "I know—we *all* know—we have a tendency to trust ourselves and the Krewe more than others. But, logically, we know those outside of the Krewe are excellent investigators and detectives, too. So, if these men are the main suspects as gathered by the inspectors here, they are probably legitimate persons of interest. But there could still be a random killer out there. All we can know—almost for sure—is that there's an underground lair somewhere. And those women are crying out before they're killed. And, Andre, a woman is still missing."

"One who might yet be saved."

"And we're..."

"Heading to a strip club. All right, if we can't get to Birmingham, we'll call Inspector Adair and suggest that he get all the volunteers needed to search, at the very least, all the catacombs and tunnels associated with the cemetery."

"He may balk. He takes his orders from Birmingham."

"Then maybe he can get to Birmingham."

They reached the Piccadilly part of the city, found parking, and walked casually, exploring the area. It was teeming with life, popular with locals and tourists alike. Neon lights advertised plays and local venues.

They stopped for fast food in the busy thoroughfare by the tinier side street that led to Pussycats and Toms.

By then, it seemed the time was right for the day workers to be off and ready for their night's pleasure.

The entrance of the club was painted a navy blue, while the outer walls were covered with pictures of the entertainment to be found within.

Missy was a blonde. Candy was a redhead. Darla was a brunette.

Andre opened the door for Cheyenne.

Inside, the club was very dark. Tables were strewn around a stage with an extension. As they entered, a scantily clad hostess greeted them and led them to her podium to choose a seating section, not seeming at all surprised that Andre had arrived with a woman. Cheyenne noted there were a few other women in the room, one standing and laughing with a man at the bar to the left of the entrance.

She didn't see Mark Bower. But they were purposely early, and the night might be long.

While the hostess asked about their table preference, Cheyenne watched the couple at the bar. The man seemed familiar.

Andre's phone buzzed, and he looked down at it.

As Cheyenne's eyes adjusted to the dark, she realized that she recognized something about the man.

When he turned, she knew why.

It was Monte Bolton, dressed now in a tweed suit.

He saw her standing there with Andre.

He quickly lowered his head, set his drink down, and moved toward the exit, leaving his companion in mid-sentence.

"Andre," Cheyenne said.

She didn't expect his response. Andre turned, saw the man, and moved after him. Monte got out the door—just barely.

Suddenly, Andre was on him, tackling Monte down to the street and straddling him before Cheyenne could reach them.

"Andre!" she said, shocked at the scene.

"Get off me!" Bolton raged.

"Sure, as soon as you admit your name isn't Monte Bolton, and you're really Inspector Birmingham!" Andre said.

Cheyenne saw Andre's phone where it lay on the ground, showing a picture Angela had just sent through. It was a photo of Inspector Claude Birmingham in full uniform.

Inspector Birmingham, who was Monte Bolton.

"Yes, damn you, I'm Birmingham!" the man on the ground raged. He struggled, still held fiercely in Andre's grasp. "And get the hell off me before I bring you in for assault and have you jailed in England for the rest of your life!"

Chapter 9

He shouldn't have lost his temper, and Andre knew it. But he felt he'd been horribly jerked around by the man, and when the picture came up on his phone just as he saw the inspector trying to slink out of the club, Andre knew he had to stop him.

For a guy who had played them so terribly, Birmingham was taking Andre's actions better than expected.

At least, now that he was standing up.

Birmingham stared at Andre, and Andre demanded, "Why?"

"I needed to know what you were about. I didn't need more crazy people running around the city, saying a vampire had arisen from Highgate!" Birmingham said. He took a breath and added, "They say you're called in for the unexplainable or the weird or…well, I'm sorry. I don't think a sixteenth or seventeenth-century count has been awakened. And I believe if there was an active cult of Satanists running around in the city, we would have noticed that by now."

"We go in to explain the unexplainable," Andre said. "Not to turn it into more legend."

"I had to know that," Birmingham said.

"Inspector, what are you doing here tonight?" Cheyenne cut in. "If you're looking for Mark Bower, I would say he will recognize you when he sees you."

"The good inspector might just be out for the night, Cheyenne," Andre said, still studying Birmingham. He wanted to trust the man, but hell, he had made fools of them.

"Watching. Just watching," Birmingham said.

"The strippers?" Andre asked.

Birmingham sighed. "People." He suddenly smiled, more like his persona of Monte Bolton. "Some of the strippers aren't bad. Sorry, but...well, I've been trying to form something of a relationship with Bower. He is still high on my list of possible killers. And I have a feeling...a *gut* feeling...that this place is somehow involved."

"Why?"

Birmingham shook his head. "No logic. The others are just...damn it, Sheila is the only one I can draw on. In investigating her, I found Mark Bower. Investigating him..." He paused to shrug. "All right, going back. Vanessa Lark spent the last several years of her life on the Continent, traveling around with money inherited from her family—all buried at Highgate. She came just to visit the cemetery. She was reported missing when the hotel where she'd been staying called it in. They couldn't find her to pay her bill, and the maid said the room hadn't been entered in a few days. Then we found her. Olivia Wordsworth had a similar story. She was down from York, split from a relationship about six months ago, and was here on holiday. Her ex-boyfriend had an ironclad alibi. The only trail we could possibly follow was that of Sheila Lynsey. Yes, we could be looking at an opportunistic killer preying on whoever he finds, but..."

"What about Edith Greenbriar?" Cheyenne asked. "She's still missing. Still out there, and the clock is ticking for her."

"Don't you think I bloody well know that?" Birmingham demanded. "I've questioned, I've talked, I've walked Swain's Lane. I've sent my men up and down the street, undercover, to check on the few possible suspects I have. Don't you think I'm aware what we're up against?" he finished in a whisper.

"Get your men out again," Andre said.

"What?"

"We believe the women are being held somewhere underground," Cheyenne said.

"Oh, right. You've been to see a few of my *gifted* friends," Birmingham said dryly. "The ground is crying. Right. Now, see, that's the very thing—"

"Not the ground, Inspector. Women. Women are being held somewhere subterranean. That, sir, would make it sound like the earth was crying."

Birmingham stared at him.

"Gentlemen," Cheyenne interrupted. "More people are coming, and they're all staring at us. We're at a strip club. I suggest we leave, or go in. And my idea is that we go in since we're here."

They both looked at her, then each other, and nodded.

When they turned, Birmingham opened the door, allowing Cheyenne and Andre entry first, then he followed.

The hostess looked a little concerned initially. But both men were stoic, and Cheyenne cheerfully asked for a table in back closer to the bar.

"Do you need to see a friend?" Cheyenne asked Birmingham. "You were with someone."

He glanced around. "She's headed back to get ready for the show." He lowered his voice. "I was talking to her about Mark Bower. Took me a while to get her to believe I wasn't after her to charge her with anything in any way. She told me his money is good—she just has to let him tie her up."

"Sounds like the man made a drastic change," Andre said.

Birmingham shrugged. "Maybe. But we don't really know about his life before. And the thing is, he may be a little on the kinkier side as far as his desires go, but—"

"Many are," Andre finished.

"And if every man who went to strip clubs—or every woman, for that matter—came under suspicion, we'd never finish with the list of suspects," Birmingham said.

Cheyenne nodded. "But you are watching Mark Bower."

"And trying to see if this club is the link. Look, the young woman you just saw has been here a long time. She's careful—she doesn't want the place closed. She knows I'm a cop hunting a murderer, but she's the only one around here who does. I trust her—as far as anyone can be trusted. A lot of the girls here go with customers—not from the club, but they make arrangements to meet them."

"Hiring prostitutes doesn't make a man a killer," Cheyenne said.

"No. But…"

Once again, Birmingham looked pained.

"I don't want to hurt the young woman," he said. "If…she's alive."

"What young woman?" Cheyenne asked.

"Edith. Edith Greenbriar," Birmingham said. He stared at them, one after the other. "Ah, bloody hell. I believe she came here, possibly looking for work."

"What?" Cheyenne raised her eyebrows in surprise. "I thought she had money."

"Doesn't mean she didn't want to live a little on the wild side," Birmingham said. "I showed her picture to Annie—Anne Connor—the woman you saw me with at the bar. I showed her all the victims and Edith Greenbriar. She said she thought Edith had been here before, but she couldn't be sure. It's still…a straw. And, yes, I'm grasping at them." He pulled out his phone as he spoke and then put through a call to his superior, asking that tunnels and any possible underground locations surrounding the cemetery be searched.

She heard a protest over the line, but Birmingham said, "Please. Yes, some of our witnesses have been bloody bats, but they might have heard something. Like screams of distress from those about to be murdered."

On the other end, someone spoke again. Birmingham glanced up at Andre and Cheyenne.

"Yes, I'm with them right now," he said. Then he ended the call. "We're in luck, mates. Some superior in the U.S. has spoken to someone here, and… I'm to help you in any way I can. And if you were part of the suggestion to search…well, then, it was a good one. Not sure if I resent that or if I'm grateful."

"We're only trying to help," Cheyenne said awkwardly.

"Right. I know," Birmingham said. "All right, I'm ready for a whiskey. What shall I get you? Something with a cherry on top, Special Agent Donegal?"

Andre laughed. "You can get me something with a cherry on top. Like a soda. I'm driving on the wrong side of the street. Cheyenne could probably use a whiskey."

"I think I should go with the soda, too."

"You're going to make me drink by myself?" Birmingham asked. "Just one. I drove out here alone."

"Then I'll have a whiskey," Cheyenne said.

He went for the drinks and returned.

His friend, Annie, went on stage in a feathery outfit that she quickly began to shed as she did calisthenics around the pole.

She was a beautiful young woman, coordinated, lithe, and sexy.

She smiled, lowering her head. Both men watched her. Of course.

Cheyenne assumed that was why she was the first to notice the man who came in and stared at the stage, oblivious to the hostess, who spoke to him for a moment.

"Don't look now," Cheyenne began softly.

"Bower?" Andre said.

"No, it's our man of optimism and faith and hope. Clark Brighton."

They both turned to look.

"What happened to don't look now?" Cheyenne asked.

"Doesn't matter. He'll recognize us," Birmingham said.

And, of course, he did. He motioned to the hostess that he just wanted to go to the bar. As he headed that way, he nearly tripped over their table in his effort to keep his gaze on Annie where she worked the pole on the stage.

"Hello, there," he said, apparently not dismayed to see them. "Enjoying our more modern London sights, eh, my friends? Inspector Birmingham."

"Didn't know you came out here, Mr. Brighton," Birmingham said.

"Clark, if you will!" He gave a little laugh, then joined them—without an invitation to do so. "Is there anything to give you more faith in life than the sight of a young woman at the height of her beauty?" He smiled at Cheyenne. "Sorry there are no men. Unless, my dear, you enjoy beauty in everyone."

"Ah, yes, beauty. She is beautiful," Cheyenne said.

"Spoken by a woman of beauty herself, I do say!" Brighton applauded. "No reason for jealousy, you are well-aware of your own loveliness. Anyway, I shall grab a drink and join you again. I am surprised to see you all together. Inspector, forgive me, but earlier, I dare say it seemed as if you didn't want us speaking with the…foreigners."

"That's changed, Mr. Brighton," Inspector Birmingham motioned to the table. "As you can see, we're having a lovely time together."

"Ah! He is more than an inspector. He is also a great tour guide!"

Brighton rose and headed to the bar. As Cheyenne watched him go, she glanced at the entry again.

Mark Bower had arrived, as well. He saw the table with their grouping and walked straight to it. "Inspector, you told me not to talk to these two, and now…liars and hypocrites, all of you. You'll never catch the killer."

"We're all watching you now, Bower," Inspector Birmingham said.

"Watching me…do what? You're going to arrest me for coming to a club?"

Bower turned to leave, telling them what they should all do with themselves in succinct terms—all perfectly pronounced with his elite London accent.

"Well, I guess tonight was…a waste of time." Birmingham turned back to his drink and the view of the stage.

"You never know," Andre said. "You weren't aware that good old Clark Brighton was a customer here until tonight, were you?"

"True," Birmingham admitted. He stood, looking at Andre and Cheyenne. "I'm going to get back and hope our search yields something."

"I guess we'll head back, too." Andre stood. "Inspector, a minute?"

"Yes?"

"Why was suspicion cast so heavily on Eric and Emily?"

"We always look at ex-boyfriends. I'm sure you and your group look for motives in murder cases, too. Eric might well have been afraid of what Sheila could do. Emily might have been jealous."

"You think a woman would have the strength to do this?" Cheyenne asked.

Birmingham leaned against the table for a minute. "What if they were working together, Special Agent Donegal? Every killer has relatives. But I do ask that you forgive me."

Cheyenne shook her head, meeting his eyes with a level stare. "No, you needn't apologize. You're doing your job. Please, keep doing it. But one more thing, if I may."

"Yes?"

"We're not the enemy."

The inspector smiled. "Several units are out scouring every conceivable piece of the underground. I do not see you as the enemy. I promise."

She nodded. With a quick return nod, he left.

Andre watched him go. "I think we should get back, too. Maybe ask if we can help."

"We're not going to catch him now," Cheyenne said.

"No. But let's head back."

"Okay."

Cheyenne noted that Annie was off the stage, and a pretty redhead with a well-endowed chest had taken over on the pole.

They started out, only to be stopped by Father Faith, who had arrived without them noticing.

"You're leaving?"

"I'm afraid so," Andre said.

"And here I thought we might have a lovely chat."

"Well, sir, exhaustion got the better of us," Cheyenne added.

"Anyway, you have a good evening."

"Oh, I will!"

He slid into the seat she had vacated. "Drive safely, my friends."

"We will, thank you," Andre assured him.

They made it out the door, only to be stopped by Annie Connor, who followed quickly in their wake, now wearing a tan trench coat over what remained of her clothing.

"You were with Claude. Claude Birmingham, right?" she asked anxiously.

"Yes," Andre said.

"It *was* Edith who was here," she said. "I didn't get a chance to tell him. He showed me a picture, and I thought it was her, but we did a silly video together, and I just brought it up. The picture he showed me didn't do her justice. But it was definitely Edith. Please…she's a lovely girl. Yes, she wanted to be a stripper, but that doesn't make a lass bad. I—"

"Please, Annie," Cheyenne interrupted. "We are not judging anyone. And no, of course, it doesn't make anyone bad."

"You have to find her."

"We will do our best," Andre promised. "I swear to you, we'll do everything in our power, and I know Inspector Birmingham will, too."

"She's still alive. I…I want to believe so badly she's still alive. I know you're American, and this is Britain, but you were with Claude. If you can help him…"

"We will do everything we can," Cheyenne assured her. She smiled. "And that includes getting back so we can help."

"Of course, of course. I'm so sorry! Go. And…thank you."

"Thank *you*," Andre told her.

They managed to head down the street to the car.

"If Edith Greenbriar is still alive, she won't be for long," Cheyenne said.

"He's draining them…but slowly. Hanging them up with just those marks…and then letting their blood drain out, bit by bit." He looked at her. "There's a chance, but…he killed Sheila right away. He may not keep Edith long at all."

"Birmingham may well be a good cop." Cheyenne thought about the inspector's motivations and decided to cut the guy some slack. "I mean, we can't really blame him for not trusting us."

"He met us, and he didn't let up on the farce," Andre said.

"True, but maybe he meant to and didn't get around to it."

He glanced her way, and she knew he was still bitter about being deceived. But could they really blame Birmingham? They weren't from here, had no connections to him, and might very well appear to be taking over in his eyes. She could understand the inspector's caution. But it seemed that he genuinely did want to solve the case and find the murderer. She just had to convince Andre to see it that way.

"Hey, he started a search."

"Because Adam Harrison called someone who called someone," Andre argued.

"I don't care how or why it happened. It's being done."

"You're right," Andre murmured.

She looked ahead as he drove, wondering why she felt discomfited. Something said that night had bothered her, but she wasn't quite sure what it was.

"You okay?" Andre asked.

She shook her head. "I feel like I should be seeing something, but whatever it is…it's just beyond my grasp."

"It'll come to you," he said softly.

"And you? Anything?"

"Yeah. Mark Bower is one of the biggest jerks I've ever come across."

She smiled. "But—"

"That doesn't make him a murderer," Andre finished.

"And," she added, grinning, "Clark Brighton likes strip clubs."

"But that doesn't make him a murderer, either."

"No. So…?"

"We get back, and we join the search," Andre said.

"If Birmingham allows it."

"He will," Andre said with assurance. She was relieved to hear it. "He will."

Chapter 10

They found Inspector Birmingham was more than happy to let them trail around after his officers, if they chose.

He was in the middle of Swain's Lane when they found him. Inspector Michael Adair was nearby and looked as if he'd been awakened from a deep sleep, but he was quick to inform them about the search thus far.

The tunnel that connected the cemeteries had been searched. They'd come up with nothing. Now, they were going through every possible vault and catacomb.

"I see you met up with your tour guide again," Adair said, grimacing.

"He's a good tour guide," Andre said lightly.

"Did you want to join any of the searchers?"

"If it's all right, we're going to take a walk along Swain's Lane and see if we see anything that might be...I don't know. Anything that might suggest another tunnel."

"Go for it," Adair told him.

"Thanks." Andre studied the lane in both directions.

"We're in the middle. Down to up, or up to down?" Cheyenne asked.

"Let's check in with your cousin. I think I see a light that way. Then we'll go down, and then all the way up again. Lots of walking...you up for it?"

She glared at him, her hands on her hips.

He put his arms up in surrender. "Right, right. You're up for anything."

"I'm just afraid, Andre. I mean, we haven't found her, and this killer doesn't mind his victims being found. So, we have a chance to save her."

He nodded. "Let's move, then."

There were indeed lights on at Emily and Eric's house—the two were obviously still awake. And some sense must have told Emily that they were coming because she stood at the door.

"Anything?" she asked anxiously.

"We got police help on the search," Cheyenne told her. "And that's good. We're heading back out, but we thought we should check in here first."

"That's sweet of you. We're doing fine. In fact, Eric is on fire. Come see what he's done!" Emily motioned for them to follow her inside.

Eric was at his laptop, which he'd set up on the dining room table. He looked up at the two of them as they arrived to see his work.

"Thank you, this is magnificent! You've got to see what I've gotten set up so far. This is really great. Bank ATM cameras only record so far. Business security systems are just for businesses. But, look! You bought the best equipment, come see what I can see!"

Cheyenne and Andre leaned over Eric's shoulders.

"You did all that with the system we bought?" Andre asked.

"Yes," Eric said. "And I was even able to activate the system's add-on night-vision capabilities without any additional equipment."

It was amazing. Eric's screen was split into boxes showing eight images. The video covered the front of the house, the back of the house, the sides, and two more angles—and then showed shots of Swain's Lane, both uphill and down.

Birmingham had gotten his superiors to call for a search, and while the street had been blocked off, just Inspector Michael Adair remained at the moment, as if he were a central point for the searchers who had gone out in all different directions.

"Wow, good work," Andre said. "I'm amazed you set all that up with what we bought."

"He is a computer whiz," Emily said proudly.

"Indeed," Andre agreed. He straightened and looked at the two of them. "We're going to head back out. I think the killer will be aware the hunt has gotten massive tonight. It could make him nervous or careless or more determined. So, please, keep yourselves locked in tight."

"We will," Emily promised, looking grim. She managed something of a smile, encouraging them to continue. "Eric has a nerd's dream here with his new toys. We will be very, very careful."

They left the house, but Cheyenne paused on the porch for a minute, waiting to hear the bolt sliding home from inside.

Andre's head was lowered, and she thought he was hiding a small smile. "Hey, you do it to me all the time—wait to see that the door is locked," she chided him.

"And the brightest people in the world sometimes get going in their heads and forget simple safety measures." He followed her to the street. "So, down and then up, right? Of course, we will be tired later. It might be easier to do up and then down."

"Nope. The house is closer to up. We'll start with down."

They headed down the lane and then back up. They didn't speak much as they watched their steps on the steep terrain.

But after they had passed Michael Adair, still standing like a sentinel, the central point for everyone out searching, Andre began to muse aloud.

"Father Faith seemed like a good guy."

"He did," Cheyenne said, fingering the little cross he had given her with the blade inside.

"But—?"

"We don't know. Benjamin Turner, charming and popular. And he cared about Sheila."

"Banker guy, Mark Bower, unlikeable," Andre said. "*Really* unlikeable."

"Bored with life, perhaps, and therefore looking for wilder pleasures."

He smiled. "Strip clubs aren't that wild."

"The club had some beautiful women. And, for your information, I have been to see the Chippendales!"

Andre laughed softly. "Okay, so, it has little to do with the fact that these suspects have been to a strip club. It's that they might have come across one another there. Or come into contact with a few of the victims."

"Random strangers. Mark Bower, Benjamin Turner, William Smith, and Clark Brighton."

"Yep."

"So, we're nowhere."

"No, we're somewhere. We have a great host of people out looking for a woman who just might still be alive."

"I haven't seen anything as we walked. Have you?"

"The night," he said softly. "Moon in the sky, some of the houses adopting decorations for Halloween—unnecessary here, really. With the brick walls, the rustle of the trees, the cemeteries on either side of us…and rumors of a vampire, along with the truths of dead bodies, they have all they need."

The path became very steep. Cheyenne leaned forward slightly to put more energy into her walking. So very much of the area was Highgate, East and West, and Waterlow Park was expansive, while Oakeshott Avenue offered homes off the path for the living. The moon afforded a whisper of light against the darkness and created shadows, as well.

To complete the tableau, Cheyenne became aware of a stereotypical London fog rolling in.

"I'm not sure how anyone can find anything here," she said bleakly.

Andre glanced her way. "You've got to be very careful, you know."

"Of course, but—"

"You're tough. You're a great agent. And I know that while I love you, I have to give you that respect, just as I give it to Angela and all our other female agents. But, Cheyenne, we're in England. Unofficially. You have amazing aim and assurance with your Glock, but we don't have our guns here."

"Birmingham has the police who are allowed to carry weapons on this," she reminded him quietly.

He nodded. "Birmingham is always with us. And I do think he believes in us—simple as that was, once we met the second time," Andre said dryly. "We'll just keep going until we find Edith Greenbriar," he added with assurance.

Cheyenne started as she saw someone step into their view, emerging out of the fog as if he were a specter himself.

It was Inspector Claude Birmingham.

Cheyenne nudged Andre. "See! Birmingham is with us," she whispered.

Andre groaned slightly.

"You two doing okay?" Birmingham asked them. "Anything?"

"A sore calf muscle," Andre said. "You?"

"Something, yes. An old tunnel. One of my men tripped and fell just outside the wall by one of those massive, old trees. He crashed down by the wall and found a covered-up hole beneath. We're combing the old records now to find out more. Once he uncovered the entry point, he was able to get into an old space that was empty but showed signs that someone had been there."

"Gum wrappers? Bottles? Something with DNA?" Andre asked hopefully.

Birmingham shook his head. "Scuff marks and old boxes. I'm not sure if the hole was part of the original plan. Maybe it was intended as a small catacomb. Or when the place was abandoned years ago, a would-be vampire-hunter managed to dig it out. Anyway, if it's there, I'm sure we'll find more. And we have a forensics team down there. Hope, as you know, springs eternal in the human heart."

"You found something," Andre said. "That absolutely means there might well be more."

Birmingham fell into step with them. "And therein lies our trouble. The area is old. London is old. Conquerors have come and gone, along with the crazed and obsessed."

Cheyenne felt her phone buzzing in her pocket.

She hung back a minute to dig it out and look at the caller I.D.

It was late, nearing two in the morning.

But it seemed that Internet sensation, Benjamin Turner, was awake.

"Hello, Donegal here," she said quickly.

"Hey, I didn't wake you, right? I heard there was a search going on. Thought you might be part of it."

"Yes, I'm awake. And, yes, we're on a search. Can I help you, or did you call because you can help *me*?"

He laughed softly. "I think I can help you."

"Then do so—please."

"You know I cater to the weird, right?" he said.

Cheyenne couldn't stop her grin. "Yes, we noticed."

"People love it. But that's all beside the point. I have done bits on Highgate Cemetery. Some just for fun, some about the exploding coffins, or about famous people—"

"Yes, yes, of course."

"Well, I went through all my old videos and found an interview I did with a fellow who was an architect."

"And?"

"He was involved with some of the construction on the high end of the lane. Anyway, he said something went on at some point in history, soon after Highgate officially opened. When he went to work, they had to change something about the foundations. We'll never know if the caverns—or catacombs—the architect claimed to have seen really existed.

Depending on what you wanted at the time, burial wasn't all that expensive. But, like today, it could cost a year's wages. He believed a group of people dug out their own caverns or vaults or whatever one wants to call them. Holes in the ground. And then, for whatever reason— maybe they were outside religion or some such thing, or just so broke they couldn't pay costs at all—they created their own catacombs. The land would have been empty or forested at the time. The area I'm talking about would be somewhere up by the new high-rise. I'm not sure how you'd go about finding them, but...I could have called the police, but they seem to think of me as the sensationalist who dated Sheila. A suspect, not someone who wants to help. And I didn't really give you anything, I suppose, but with those search parties out there, maybe you have some sway."

Yes, thankfully, they did have some sway.

And while the fog closed in, and she hung back to make the call private, she could hear Birmingham and Andre talking quietly up ahead.

Ghostly shapes moved through the fog around them.

"Definitely, Benjamin. I believe they're listening to us now. I'm just behind Inspector Birmingham and Andre currently. We've felt certain the killer has a hiding place where he...drains his victims. We've been thinking underground, but you've given us some direction. You've been a tremendous help."

"I should have been on this bloody damned case sooner. I've spent so much time in Highgate Cemetery doing bits, and every time with the best tour guides."

"Well, thank you. We'll get on it."

Cheyenne hung up, ready to hurry forward to tell Andre and Birmingham what Benjamin had told her.

Words suddenly swam in her head.

Tour guide.

Birmingham had pretended to be a tour guide.

And this evening...

Someone had mentioned that. Someone who shouldn't have known about it.

She opened her mouth, ready to hurry ahead.

And then she felt it. Hard, searing pain on the top of her skull.

The moon's light faded. The fog swam all around her.

And then, darkness was complete.

Chapter 11

"We're grateful that you're doing this. I honestly believe we have a chance of finding Edith Greenbriar alive," Andre told Birmingham.

"You're grateful? It's my job," Birmingham said and looked up at the sky. "The fog has come in heavy tonight. But if we're underground, it may not matter. I've had men everywhere, but you're right, we found a big hole we knew nothing about. We can bloody well find another." He hesitated. "I guess I should have listened more to Clark Brighton. But you understand, we deal with what's real. I'll ask you to understand that with all the hauntings and vampire talk—'the earth is moaning' indeed!—he just sounded like another fanatic. It didn't occur to me that people might be held captive beneath the ground. And, yes, they'd be moaning and screaming. How did you come to that? Isn't it flatland where you come from? We hear about flooding over there."

"Ah, yes, we have our share of stories in New Orleans. I think this one was made up, but as the story goes, a woman and her husband in the first half of the nineteenth century practiced horrible medical experiments on their patients. A maid committed suicide, and then a cook set fire to the house—all to escape. They succeeded, and then the ghost stories started up. Only one tale had it where people heard the living who had been imprisoned in a tomb in the courtyard, not the sound of ghosts crying. True or not, I don't know, but with this terrain…anyway, Cheyenne might be more up on the story than me." Looking back, he added, "Cheyenne, do you know more about that NOLA story?"

She didn't answer.

He strained to see through the fog.

"Cheyenne?"

Birmingham looked concerned, as well. "She was right there, just behind us, seconds ago." He drew out his flashlight, a powerful one, and played it over the lane behind them.

There was no sign of Cheyenne.

Andre shouted her name and ran back in the direction from which they had come.

Nothing. No one.

Just fog.

He pulled out his phone, calling hers.

It rang and rang and rang.

"Andre—sorry, Special Agent Rousseau, don't panic, the lady likely just saw something and stepped off," Birmingham said.

But Andre didn't believe that. "We were right damned in front of her!"

As in the days of old, the policeman carried a whistle. He blew on it, drawing out his phone as he did.

"Cheyenne!" Andre cried again, now running. When he realized he was running in circles, he stopped to think more logically. He was certain she hadn't hopped a wall. They would have heard that.

In seconds, a score of men came running toward them.

Birmingham announced that they were changing up the search. Cheyenne Donegal had just disappeared—from right behind them. She had to be close. She *had* to be.

And they weren't to stop looking until they found her.

Andre fought hard to keep himself from growing frantic. He needed to stay calm and focused.

But he despised himself for being an idiot, for not keeping her immediately at his side while they walked, while they worked...

"I need to get ahold of our phone company, quickly. I need to know who called her last," Andre said. "They can do it faster in the States, I'm..."

He shook his head and pulled out his cell, calling Angela, telling her briefly and tersely what was going on, and leaving her to find the last call on Cheyenne's phone.

Then he started running again.

"Where are you going?" Birmingham demanded, following behind him.

"Eric and Emily's," he said. "The camera...it might show this far down the lane, and they might have seen what happened. Something, anything."

Birmingham kept in step with him. They passed Michael Adair, still sitting vigil, and Birmingham shouted orders to him, making sure every man and woman on the job knew that Cheyenne had just disappeared.

They were all out here tonight.

And so was a killer.

Andre pounded on the door at the house and immediately pushed past Emily when she opened it, Birmingham following behind him.

"Andre! What—?"

"Cheyenne," he said, making his way to the dining room.

Eric had fallen asleep in the parlor just beyond, but he heard Andre, and—though a little dazed—rose with a smile that quickly faded.

"The footage. Go back, Eric. Go back and bring up the cameras that are recording video on the lane!"

"Yes, yes, of course," Eric started typing.

"Cheyenne? Cheyenne—what?" Emily demanded. And then, "Oh, my God," she whispered.

Because Eric had brought up the screens of the lane.

And, through the fog, they could see two dark figures.

Andre and Birmingham, walking together.

And behind them...

A tall figure wearing a cloak—one that almost blended in with the night—coming up quickly and silently, right behind Cheyenne.

The figure struck her. Swept her up.

Ran back with her in his arms...

Out of the camera's view.

"Oh, my God!" Emily wept.

Andre's phone rang. It was Angela.

"She spoke with Benjamin Turner," Angela said.

"Thanks."

He said no more and hung up, looking at Birmingham as he rang through to Turner.

"Did you find something?" Turner demanded. "I was telling Cheyenne about what I learned looking back and—"

"What did you tell her? What did you tell her?" Andre demanded. He saw his fingers where he gripped the phone. They were white with tension.

He couldn't panic. He had to stay sane, think logically.

"I interviewed an architect. He said they had to make changes to the plans. Didn't know how or when, but someone dug out tombs that aren't in the cemetery. They're now on what I assume is private land by the new apartments. According to him, no one reported the remains to the proper authorities because it would have delayed the construction."

Birmingham waited.

Andre tensed.

What if Turner's information was interesting but had nothing to do with Cheyenne's abduction?

Andre closed his eyes for a second and breathed deeply.

Cheyenne was a trained agent.

But she'd been slammed in the head, knocked out.

This murderer didn't kill quickly, though. He bled his victims out.

There was time. And Andre had to use it.

"Thanks," he said briefly to Turner, hanging up even as Turner kept speaking, asking if they had managed to find anything.

"Up a slope, by the new apartments," he said. "Turner found an interview with a guy who suggested that, at some point in time, someone dug out their own catacombs."

Birmingham nodded. He had his phone out and was calling his teams, telling them where to concentrate their searches.

Birmingham started for the door with Andre behind him but stopped abruptly. "What if...what if Benjamin Turner is the killer? What if he called Cheyenne to distract her, to get her to hang back?"

"Can you get a man there quickly?"

"Within minutes."

"Let's head on toward the new apartments. Get someone to see if Turner is at his place. If he took her, he'd have to have superpowers to stash her and be back sipping tea at home already."

"I'll get someone to his flat immediately. Of course, he could have her at his place, just holding on until we get out of the way. We have laws here, and we can't just go bursting in without—"

"You can't. But I can. I'm an unofficial agent here. An American," Andre said.

"Let's go see what else he has."

"Get your men up by the new apartments. Every girder, every patch of dirt, in the basement, in the gardens...everywhere." Andre said.

"I have a car ahead—with a siren."

Andre was grateful that Birmingham had his car—and his siren.

They moved through Highgate like lightning.

He thought about the evening. He tried to replay every word, remembered that something had been said during the night that had bothered Cheyenne. She'd said as much. It wasn't something she could put her finger on, though. He'd told her not to worry, that it would come to her.

They reached Benjamin Turner's place. He opened the door wearing a silk smoking jacket, seemingly surprised to see them.

"Where is she?" Andre demanded.

"What? Who?"

"Cheyenne!"

Birmingham stepped in behind him. "Mr. Turner, we need to ask you a few questions, and we need your help—"

Andre didn't hear any more. He walked past the foyer with its reception area and desk and into the room where he had so recently sat with Turner and Cheyenne. He burst into the studio, returned to the parlor, and looked down the hallway at the closed doors of other rooms.

Behind him, he heard Turner telling Birmingham that he was free to search—everywhere.

And they did. Quickly. From the basement to the attic.

Everywhere.

And it was while Andre stood in the parlor, frustrated, that something struck him.

A memory. Recollection of a conversation.

He turned to Benjamin Turner.

"Do you have that footage you mentioned?"

"Of course, I was just watching it."

"Did the architect have the original plans? Are they on the video at all?"

"I—I'll bring it up and see," Turner said.

He walked into his studio to do so. They followed.

On screen, the architect was a lean man in his thirties, eager to be interviewed on-air for one of Benjamin's popular bits of history and culture.

He talked about his feelings regarding the construction of such a blatantly modern building in the middle of so much history.

And yet, the world moved on. Land was for the living. Still, while he shouldn't be sharing what he was sharing…

The construction was done. And everyone knew Highgate was spooky as all hell already.

He did have the plans. They were right there on the screen.

Andre took a step forward and pointed. "Stop! Freeze frame and print. Can you?"

"Oh, aye, easy enough!" Turner told him.

In seconds, Andre had several pages of original plans.

And blueprints of the buildings as they stood now.

His "thank you" was brief.

In a minute, he was back out the door, impatiently remembering that Birmingham had driven, and he had to wait for him.

Thankfully, the inspector was right behind him.

"To the bloody apartments. We're going to find her, my friend. We're going to find her. And have faith. She's trained. She..."

"She's unarmed. And she was knocked out," Andre said, staring ahead.

"We have the plans—"

"You didn't know anything about these unauthorized catacombs?" Andre asked.

"Oh, good God, every damned tree in England was a hanging tree! Every parking lot covers a grave. Good Lord, man, if I'd known..."

"We'll find her," Andre said, determined. Then he turned to Birmingham and added, "We'll find her, and we'll stop him. Because I know now."

"You know—"

"I know who the killer is."

Chapter 12

Cheyenne remembered. She remembered it all.

Everything that had led to her being here, hanging by her wrists, her arms shooting out agonizing lightning bolts of pain, her head as heavy as an anvil.

But that was nothing.

Cheyenne had found Edith Greenbriar.

Edith Greenbriar was hanging by her ankles next to her.

Drip. Drip.

And yet...

She strained to see in the poor light that filtered through the catacombs. Somewhere, someone had a lantern set up, or a powerful flashlight turned on. Not in the immediate area, but somewhere near.

The catacombs must stretch on. England had a long history. A lot of people had died throughout the centuries, most without even the small amount needed for a decent burial or interment when Highgate first opened.

Think!

Yes, she had found Edith Greenbriar. And while the woman's lifeblood was drip, drip, dripping from her body, there was a slim chance that she was still alive.

And in need of saving.

Cheyenne needed to be saved herself.

Andre would figure it out—as *she* had figured it out. She had faith in him, as he had in her.

That night…

She had been a little too late. And she might be wrong.

But she wasn't.

Inspector Birmingham had played a trick on them when they first arrived. He'd pretended to be a tour guide so he could observe them.

But he surely hadn't made that public knowledge.

Michael Adair had known. He had been part of the prank.

But Clark Brighton shouldn't have had any reason to know. And, that night, he had laughed at the table about Inspector Birmingham being a great tour guide.

He knew…because he had followed them.

He'd been so helpful…

Telling them about the way the earth was moaning, knowing that most people would think him a madman, a so-called wiseman, a New Age priest!

He'd followed them back, and he'd known they'd be searching. And then he'd stayed behind and bided his time. Until now…

Cheyenne looked up. The ties holding her were rope. If she could just get one hand free…

She would rip the hell out of her wrist.

Better that than being hung up like a stuck pig.

She began working at the knots, remembering the little pendant William Smith, good Father Faith, had given her.

It hung around her neck.

Concentrate, concentrate, concentrate…

The pain was almost unbearable, but finally…

The blood helped. She slipped her right wrist free and ripped the pendant from around her throat.

Then she used the tiny, razor-sharp blade to free her left wrist.

She felt herself falling to the floor. Her breath caught, but she moved quickly to right herself, lest the fall alert her captor to the fact that she was free.

Maybe he was already gone. She doubted it. He'd be back to see if Edith Greenbriar was dead yet and ready to be set out somewhere on the lane, possibly near a jack-o-lantern or some other Halloween decoration.

A macabre display encouraging the legend of the Highgate vampire.

It wasn't going to happen. She wouldn't let it happen.

Edith was strung high by her ankles, causing the blood to drip, drip, drip slowly from the puncture wounds—the fang marks—on her neck.

She was unconscious, but she seemed to be alive.

Barely.

Cheyenne had to get her down swiftly.

The hook that held Edith's bindings was high. Cheyenne wouldn't be able to reach the ropes without help.

She winced, seeing the edge of a broken coffin on a low shelf, halfway lying on the floor.

She hurried to it and, with painstaking care, edged it over to where she could stand on it.

The lid was partly rotted, and she could see the cadaverous face of the coffin's occupant inside, skin stretched tight over bone in a grisly mask.

She looked away and carefully tested her weight.

The edges seemed mostly solid. She crawled up on top of the coffin and could just reach the ropes. The blade in the cross was small but sharp. She sawed and sawed, and the rope began to give. When it did, she realized the weight of the woman, though not great, would bring her down the rest of the way. Cheyenne had to be ready.

And she was. But she teetered dangerously on the coffin's edge before finally managing an almost silent leap to the ground.

The weight did her in, though. She fell, with Edith Greenbriar atop her.

For a moment, she lay still and silent, listening. She could hear bits of movement. Clark Brighton was still in the mire of the catacombs somewhere.

She had to keep quiet. Find a weapon, bide her time.

Andre would come. He would have checked on her last phone call, and he'd have gone to or talked to Benjamin Turner.

He was near. He had to be.

She eased herself out from under the body of Edith Greenbriar.

Cutting a piece of material from her sweater, she pressed it against the puncture wounds on the woman's neck.

She didn't know if it was enough.

She grabbed the woman's wrist to check for a pulse, hoping she wasn't desperately trying to save a corpse.

Miraculously, she found it. The tiniest hint of life.

But she needed help fast. Edith required medical care. Immediately.

Very carefully, Cheyenne came to her feet and looked around. She needed a weapon other than the tiny blade in her cross. Using that would require her to get closer than she felt comfortable with.

Suddenly, she saw something she never expected to see. A figure, but not that of her captor. It was Lady Elizabeth, coming through the doorway of the room. She held a finger to her lips, signaling for Cheyenne to remain quiet, but pointed at the coffin near her.

Cheyenne moved closer and glanced down. The corpse inside was mostly decayed. And his bones...

She couldn't do it.

Hell, yes, she could.

She glanced up to thank the ghost, but she was once again alone in the chamber with Edith. Elizabeth Miller was nowhere to be seen.

Cheyenne's decision for whether or not to desecrate a corpse to get herself out of this mess was made almost instantly because, even as she pondered it, Clark Brighton came walking into that section of the catacombs.

He startled when he saw her, but carried that same gold golf club he'd used to deck her before.

* * * *

"So, who is it? What the hell is going on?" Birmingham demanded, glancing at Andre.

"Clark Brighton," Andre said.

"That old—?"

"Not that old. Strong. And powerful. And he lives in the new apartments. He might have stumbled upon the crypt or catacombs or whatever at some point, or he might have found the original plans and compared them to what was built...or watched one of Benjamin Turner's Internet shows and found out that way. Who knows? But it's perfect. I just wonder if..."

"If?"

Andre looked at Birmingham.

"I wonder if he is working alone."

"Don't you be looking at me that way!" Birmingham said explosively. "No way in bloody hell would I ever think to hurt another living soul. Sir—"

"Hey, stop! I wasn't referring to you. Here's the thing. Somehow, Clark Brighton knew you pretended to be the tour guide to meet us."

"Now, there you go again. Michael Adair is as fine an inspector as have ever known. There is no cause—"

"I didn't suggest Inspector Adair, either. I believe Clark Brighton followed us and saw you. But I still wonder if he's in this alone."

Birmingham was silent.

They had reached the apartments. Others followed behind them. Some of Birmingham's men were already moving to the building itself.

"He could have carried it off. He's a big man, a powerful one. It's easy enough to take a small woman. And, as you learned, he's easy to trust."

"He wanted us all to believe Satanists were at work, but he's the leader of beauty and peace and softness in the air. I fell for the bastard's bullshit."

"You're sure it's him?"

"Pretty damned sure. But we'll find out soon enough. We *will* find Cheyenne, and we'll find her soon."

Birmingham fell silent.

Andre knew the man was hoping that they found her alive.

"Well, he usually displays his victims one at a time, and we haven't come upon Edith Greenbriar's body yet," Birmingham said. Then he winced.

Finding another woman dead was a bitter thought.

"I'm still wondering about…the other women. Except for Sheila, they were held for a time before they were found. That makes me think two people might have been involved, as well. One who was impatient, and one who was not."

"And Clark Brighton—"

"He liked the process. Keeping the women, draining them slowly."

"So, the unknown accomplice killed Sheila?"

"Possibly."

"Possibly. You're right," Birmingham said.

As they talked, they studied the terrain and the maps. And Andre thought he'd been heading in the right direction, but…

As he looked up, he saw something. A figure moved in the fog—at least, he thought he saw something—but then it disappeared as if it had vanished into thin air.

Or fell into the earth.

Another, dimmer figure followed but didn't disappear. Instead, it came closer.

And Andre saw her, saw her clearly. It was Lady Elizabeth Miller, and she was beckoning madly, pointing to the place where the other person had disappeared.

Andre started to run.

"Hey!" Birmingham called.

"There, by the tree! There's a bush by it that's...crooked. It's probably where a foundation should have been started. Come on!"

* * * *

"Well, look at you, Miss Bloody Hot-Stuff American agent!" Clark Brighton said, smiling—apparently not displeased that she had worked her way down, likely happy to have a go at her again.

"You bloody bastard!" she yelled. "All talk of the air and the earth and goodness and light. You knew damned well the screams and moans you heard were your victims. And you hoped the police would go crazy right in the cemetery."

He smiled. "They did."

"And you enjoyed it."

"Loved it! Loved talking to the good Inspectors Birmingham and Adair and letting them know what a harmless idiot I was."

"They aren't fools, Mr. Brighton. You were on their suspect list."

He frowned at that. "Bloody idiots."

"Again, I beg to differ. They were on to you, which is why *we* were on to you."

"A little too late, though, eh, missy? I'd like to take some time with you, but...ah, well, upside down, bleeding out, you might not be so clever. How is our Miss Greenbriar doing? Is she ready for disposal yet? Did you save the dead?" he asked her.

Cheyenne smiled, judging the size of her thigh-bone weapon against his golf club.

She needed him off guard. She'd had training, but he was big and powerful. *Balance*, she reminded herself. Balance and fighting with the mind, conserving strength.

"No," she said cheerfully. "She's still breathing."

"Not for long, I dare say."

"Do you know how sick you are?" she asked him.

He shook his head and grew serious. "Sick? No. I'm ridding the world of the riff-raff, my dear girl, and making it safe for God-fearing men again."

"What?"

"Wretches, horrid little creatures. Evil. Each deserved to die, to have their blood drench the earth."

"You're crazier than I thought."

"Not crazy! Offended. Insulted by women of loose morals. You think you know, but you do not! And you...as wretched as any of them. Worse. You think you are equal to a man? I'll show you! Tonight's going to be the best Blood Night ever."

He was, beyond a doubt, crazier than she had thought.

But she'd done what was needed. She had riled his temper to a point where he would come at her in a fury.

He lunged as expected, golf club swinging.

She let him use his own weight and momentum against himself and swept to the side with a split second to spare. The club crashed down on the coffin, carrying the weight of his arm and shoulder with it.

She raised her thigh bone high and slammed it down on his head for all she was worth.

Good aim, a direct hit.

He went down, groaning, and then lay still.

She hit him one more time, hard, for good measure.

That wasn't from any FBI training. That was from watching far too many horror and crime movies where the bad guy was trounced—only to get up again.

She moved quickly in the direction from which he had come, the thigh bone still in her hand. The entry to the catacombs had to be somewhere over there, and she had to get out and get help for Edith. Fast.

She followed the light into a second space, the outer room of the catacomb chambers.

A coffin had been used as a table. Clark Brighton had set his lantern there. She could see that there was a little ladder beyond it.

It had to lead to a hatch of some kind.

She ran toward the ladder.

Then, suddenly, the hatch opened. Before she could go farther, a man jumped down and landed before her.

This might be England, but he had a gun.

And it was aimed directly at her.

She backed away slowly, knowing now that Clark Brighton had a partner.

And after the night she'd had, the partner's identity wasn't surprising. Some of Andre's instincts had been right.

"Ah, Mr. Bower," she said. "Why am I not surprised? Let's see…Sheila appeared almost immediately after being killed because she hurt your sense of masculinity. Am I right? Brighton slowly killed the others—with you, in whatever your macho ritual was—but *you* killed Sheila. Because she hurt your little feelings, right?"

"You're going to die so much faster than she did, Special Agent Bitch!" he said, raising the gun.

It never fired.

Andre leapt down on top of him, and the gun went flying out of Bower's hand.

They weren't in the United States. They were Americans, unofficially in Britain. Andre was just a provoked tourist, caught in a violent situation…

Andre landed hard on Bower. Slammed him to the floor, wrenched him over, and sent a right hook flying into his jaw that seemed to affect the entire catacombs.

Indeed, a coffin rattled precariously on a shelf.

Another man landed in the catacomb tunnel. Birmingham.

"Give him one for me, too, won't you?" Birmingham asked.

But she saw Andre wince and then stand. "Sorry, friend. He's already out cold. And if you don't mind…"

He took a step toward Cheyenne and pulled her into his arms and held her.

After they'd felt each other's heartbeats and were reassured that they were both alive and well and…together, he pulled away.

"Clark Brighton?" he asked her anxiously.

"Next room. With Edith. We have to get help immediately. She's still alive, but barely. Oh, my God, if we move fast enough—"

"On it!" Brighton told them, his phone already out.

He called for help and, in just seconds, medical personnel flooded into the catacombs. She and Andre and the inspector moved aside to make room.

"You knocked out Clark Brighton?" Birmingham asked her.

"Corpse's thigh bone," she said.

"Ah," Birmingham said, looking at Andre. "So, uh, she took out one, and you got the other?"

Andre laughed. "Something like that," he said. "And if we may…"

"Get out! Get help. You should have your wrist looked at," he said, pointing at her hand where blood still leaked from the torn flesh above it.

"I will, I will!" Cheyenne promised. "But now..."

Birmingham moved the little ladder, reaching to give her a hand.

"Oh, uh, if I may?" he asked.

"Always happy for an assist," she told him, and she couldn't help herself. She paused, giving him a smile and a hug before she headed up and out of the tunnel. "Always grateful for help. And courtesy. And decency among all men and women."

He smiled at her. "My kind of agent," he said. "Both of you." He tipped his chin at Andre.

Andre thanked him and followed Cheyenne up the ladder.

She felt his arms around her as they emerged.

The sun was just rising, bursting through the fog and the darkness of the night.

The day was going to be beautiful.

Epilogue

"You have to listen well, man," Michael Adair said. He shook his head. "You can't tell the Irish from the Scottish? Ah, the first is a lilt, it goes up and down. Beautifully melodic. The second has that burring sound to it, not so musical."

"He's only saying that," Claude Birmingham assured them, "because his dad came here from Dublin, and my mother came from Scotland. The Scots' accent is soft and sweet and pure as a whisper against oak!"

"Uh…they're both lovely," Cheyenne said, quickly adding, "as is the English accent." She glanced at Eric, who was at the table, too, along with Emily and Andre.

The inspectors had stopped by to tell them that, miraculously, Edith Greenbriar was going to live, and she wanted to see them.

"And don't bother telling me you did nothing to deserve gratitude," Birmingham had said. "Miss Greenbriar considers her life extremely valuable. You should be thanked for saving it."

She and Andre had agreed to go by the hospital.

But they were also heading out.

"Back to the U.S.A. for Halloween, eh?" Adair asked.

"No!" they told him in unison, and Cheyenne laughed and explained. "Costa del Sol. Vacation!"

"Ah, lovely," Birmingham said.

The men had agreed to take a minute for a cup of tea and a few sandwiches before moving on. There was still paperwork to be done, a press conference to be held, and convincing the public that a vampire had not been roaming around Highgate.

"Well, like, you know, don't you? There's far more than one English accent," Eric teased in a funny tone, perfectly mimicking a valley girl accent.

"And yet we all say 'vampire' just about the same way," Emily noted. "When chasing one and not fooling around, anyway." She shivered. "I can't believe it's really over."

"It's really over," Birmingham told her. "And please forgive us. But we did follow whatever leads we could find."

"You're forgiven. I got to see my cousin and meet Eric!"

"Such a loss…all those women. Did Brighton and Bower really go so crazy because they had their feelings hurt somewhere along the line?" Eric asked.

"Clark Brighton? I think he truly is a narcissistic psychopath with no sense of empathy whatsoever. A man who enjoyed what he did just to see if he could do it. He fell in with Mark Bower—who was bitter. Sheila was, sadly, the final straw for him. The men met and discovered they were a lethal pair. As to the whole of it, we'll be sorting it out for a long time. I mean, we still don't know why they chose you as their scapegoats. Why they tried to set you up. But we have some time to get to the bottom of everything. I seriously doubt that either of them will ever see the outside of a prison again," Birmingham assured.

"We're getting commendations," Adair said. "They belong to you two, as well."

Andre shook his head. "We followed your leads. And, hey, an alliance is always best, right?"

Birmingham laughed. "Ah, bloody hell, I guess we do best now when we get along with the colonials, right, Michael?"

"Yes. And we thank you," he said.

"We thank *you*," Cheyenne assured him. "Oh, and for the tour, too."

"I guess if all else fails, I could be a guide," Birmingham said with a grin. "Glad you enjoyed it."

He stood, and Michael Adair stood with him. The two headed out.

When they were gone, Emily asked anxiously, "Are you leaving right away? One more dinner would be lovely, and I'm sure the flights in the morning—"

"We're having dinner here, Emily," Andre said, interrupting her. "But," he added, looking at Cheyenne, "we have to go out for just a few minutes this morning. We'll pop by the hospital quickly after, then come back for dinner and the night. We'll take off in the morning."

"Lovely!" Emily said.

Cheyenne thought she knew where Andre wanted to go, and she was right.

They paid their fee and wandered into Highgate Cemetery, just strolling along, admiring the beauty of the foliage and the tombs.

"I hope we see her," Cheyenne said.

"We will," Andre said with assurance.

And they did.

They were alone on the trail when they spotted her, Lady Elizabeth Miller, heading their way, a smile on her face.

"I wish I could hug you!" Cheyenne told her.

"I shall try to hug you!" the ghost said.

Cheyenne saw her move and felt a cool breeze as the ghost stepped up to her, trying for a warm embrace. It was a little chilly, in truth, but...

"How was that?" Elizabeth asked.

"Lovely. The best ever. You saved my life," Cheyenne said.

"Ah, well, you saved that poor Edith. I only pointed out a possible weapon and saw Mark Bower heading for the tomb later. Andre would have found the entrance eventually, with or without me—"

"I don't know how a banker got a gun in England, but he had one—and it was aimed right at my heart. Andre told me you were there just in time," Cheyenne said.

"You were," Andre agreed.

"So, I did save a life!" Elizabeth said happily. "I saved a life!"

"Two lives."

Cheyenne noted then that Elizabeth wasn't alone haunting the cemetery.

When she looked back to a rise where a multitude of crooked headstones came down from a mausoleum, she saw several shadowy forms in all manner of dress, spanning many decades.

"I think your friends want to congratulate you," Andre said. He waved to the small crowd of spirits, blowing a kiss.

She headed up the hill.

Andre smiled at Cheyenne. She grinned in return and took his proffered hand.

Together, they walked out of Highgate.

Envisioning the Costa del Sol beaches.

* * * *

Also from 1001 Dark Nights and Heather Graham, discover Haunted Be the Holidays, Hallow Be The Haunt, Crimson Twilight, When Irish Eyes Are Haunting, All Hallows Eve, and Blood on the Bayou.

Sign up for the 1001 Dark Nights Newsletter
and be entered to win a Tiffany Key necklace.

There's a contest every month!

Go to www.1001DarkNights.com to subscribe.

**As a bonus, all subscribers can download
FIVE FREE exclusive books!**

Discover 1001 Dark Nights Collection Six

Go to www.1001DarkNights.com for more information.

DRAGON CLAIMED by Donna Grant
A Dark Kings Novella

ASHES TO INK by Carrie Ann Ryan
A Montgomery Ink: Colorado Springs Novella

ENSNARED by Elisabeth Naughton
An Eternal Guardians Novella

EVERMORE by Corinne Michaels
A Salvation Series Novella

VENGEANCE by Rebecca Zanetti
A Dark Protectors/Rebels Novella

ELI'S TRIUMPH by Joanna Wylde
A Reapers MC Novella

CIPHER by Larissa Ione
A Demonica Underworld Novella

RESCUING MACIE by Susan Stoker
A Delta Force Heroes Novella

ENCHANTED by Lexi Blake
A Masters and Mercenaries Novella

TAKE THE BRIDE by Carly Phillips
A Knight Brothers Novella

INDULGE ME by J. Kenner
A Stark Ever After Novella

THE KING by Jennifer L. Armentrout
A Wicked Novella

QUIET MAN by Kristen Ashley
A Dream Man Novella

ABANDON by Rachel Van Dyken
A Seaside Pictures Novella

THE OPEN DOOR by Laurelin Paige
A Found Duet Novella

CLOSER by Kylie Scott
A Stage Dive Novella

SOMETHING JUST LIKE THIS by Jennifer Probst
A Stay Novella

BLOOD NIGHT by Heather Graham
A Krewe of Hunters Novella

TWIST OF FATE by Jill Shalvis
A Heartbreaker Bay Novella

MORE THAN PLEASURE YOU by Shayla Black
A More Than Words Novella

WONDER WITH ME by Kristen Proby
A With Me In Seattle Novella

THE DARKEST ASSASSIN by Gena Showalter
A Lords of the Underworld Novella

Also from 1001 Dark Nights:
DAMIEN by J. Kenner

Discover More Heather Graham

✳Haunted Be the Holidays: A Krewe of Hunters Novella

When you're looking for the victim of a mysterious murder in a theater, there is nothing like calling on a dead diva for help! Krewe members must find the victim if they're to discover the identity of a murderer at large, one more than willing to kill the performers when he doesn't like the show.

It's Halloween at the Global Tower Theatre, a fantastic and historic theater owned by Adam Harrison and run by spouses of Krewe members. During a special performance, a strange actor makes an appearance in the middle of the show, warning of dire events if his murder is not solved before another holiday rolls around.

Dakota McCoy and Brodie McFadden dive into the mystery. Both have a. special talent for dealing with ghosts, but this one is proving elusive. With the help of Brodie's diva mother and his ever-patient father—who were killed together when a stage chandelier fell upon them—Dakota and Brodie set out to solve the case.

If they can't solve the murder quickly, there will be no Thanksgiving for the Krewe...

* * * *

✳Hallow Be the Haunt: A Krewe of Hunters Novella

Years ago, Jake Mallory fell in love all over again with Ashley Donegal—while he and the Krewe were investigating a murder that replicated a horrible Civil War death at her family's Donegal Plantation.

Now, Ashley and Jake are back—planning for their wedding, which will take place the following month at Donegal Plantation, her beautiful old antebellum home.

But Halloween is approaching and Ashley is haunted by a ghost warning her of deaths about to come in the city of New Orleans, deaths caused by the same murderer who stole the life of the beautiful ghost haunting her dreams night after night.

At first, Jake is afraid that returning home has simply awakened some of the fear of the past…

But as Ashley's nightmares continue, a body count begins to accrue in the city…

And it's suddenly a race to stop a killer before Hallow's Eve comes to a crashing end, with dozens more lives at stake, not to mention heart, soul, and life for Jake and Ashley themselves.

* * * *

Crimson Twilight: A Krewe of Hunters Novella

It's a happy time for Sloan Trent and Jane Everett. What could be happier than the event of their wedding? Their Krewe friends will all be there and the event will take place in a medieval castle transported brick by brick to the New England coast. Everyone is festive and thrilled… until the priest turns up dead just hours before the nuptials. Jane and Sloan must find the truth behind the man and the murder--the secrets of the living and the dead--before they find themselves bound for eternity--not in wedded bliss but in the darkness of an historical wrong and their own brutal deaths.

* * * *

When Irish Eyes Are Haunting: A Krewe of Hunters Novella

Devin Lyle and Craig Rockwell are back, this time to a haunted castle in Ireland where a banshee may have gone wild—or maybe there's a much more rational explanation—one that involves a disgruntled heir, murder, and mayhem, all with that sexy light touch Heather Graham has turned into her trademark style.

* * * *

All Hallows Eve: A Krewe of Hunters Novella

Salem was a place near and dear to Jenny Duffy and Samuel Hall -- it was where they'd met on a strange and sinister case. They never dreamed that they'd be called back. That history could repeat itself in a most macabre and terrifying fashion. But, then again, it was Salem at

Halloween. Seasoned Krewe members, they still find themselves facing the unspeakable horrors in a desperate race to save each other-and perhaps even their very souls.

* * * *

Blood on the Bayou: A Cafferty & Quinn Novella

It's winter and a chill has settled over the area near New Orleans, finding a stream of blood, a tourist follows it to a dead man, face down in the bayou.

The man has been done in by a vicious beating, so violent that his skull has been crushed in.

It's barely a day before a second victim is found... once again so badly thrashed that the water runs red. The city becomes riddled with fear.

An old family friend comes to Danni Cafferty, telling her that he's terrified, he's certain that he's received a message from the Blood Bayou killer--It's your turn to pay, blood on the bayou.

Cafferty and Quinn quickly become involved, and--as they all begin to realize that a gruesome local history is being repeated--they find themselves in a fight to save not just a friend, but, perhaps, their very own lives.

About Heather Graham

New York Times and USA Today bestselling author, Heather Graham, majored in theater arts at the University of South Florida. After a stint of several years in dinner theater, back-up vocals, and bartending, she stayed home after the birth of her third child and began to write. Her first book was with Dell, and since then, she has written over two hundred novels and novellas including category, suspense, historical romance, vampire fiction, time travel, occult and Christmas family fare.

She is pleased to have been published in approximately twenty-five languages. She has written over 200 novels and has 60 million books in print. She has been honored with awards from booksellers and writers' organizations for excellence in her work, and she is also proud to be a recipient of the Silver Bullet from Thriller Writers and was also awarded the prestigious Thriller Master in 2016. She is also a recipient of the Lifetime Achievement Award from RWA. Heather has had books selected for the Doubleday Book Club and the Literary Guild, and has been quoted, interviewed, or featured in such publications as The Nation, Redbook, Mystery Book Club, People and USA Today and appeared on many newscasts including Today, Entertainment Tonight and local television.

Heather loves travel and anything that has to do with the water and is a certified scuba diver. She also loves ballroom dancing. Each year she hosts the Vampire Ball and Dinner theater at the RT convention raising money for the Pediatric Aids Society and in 2006 she hosted the first Writers for New Orleans Workshop to benefit the stricken Gulf Region. She is also the founder of "The Slush Pile Players," presenting something that's "almost like entertainment" for various conferences and benefits. Married since high school graduation and the mother of five, her greatest love in life remains her family, but she also believes her career has been an incredible gift, and she is grateful every day to be doing something that she loves so very much for a living.

Discover 1001 Dark Nights

Go to www.1001DarkNights.com for more information.

COLLECTION ONE
FOREVER WICKED by Shayla Black
CRIMSON TWILIGHT by Heather Graham
CAPTURED IN SURRENDER by Liliana Hart
SILENT BITE: A SCANGUARDS WEDDING by Tina Folsom
DUNGEON GAMES by Lexi Blake
AZAGOTH by Larissa Ione
NEED YOU NOW by Lisa Renee Jones
SHOW ME, BABY by Cherise Sinclair
ROPED IN by Lorelei James
TEMPTED BY MIDNIGHT by Lara Adrian
THE FLAME by Christopher Rice
CARESS OF DARKNESS by Julie Kenner

COLLECTION TWO
WICKED WOLF by Carrie Ann Ryan
WHEN IRISH EYES ARE HAUNTING by Heather Graham
EASY WITH YOU by Kristen Proby
MASTER OF FREEDOM by Cherise Sinclair
CARESS OF PLEASURE by Julie Kenner
ADORED by Lexi Blake
HADES by Larissa Ione
RAVAGED by Elisabeth Naughton
DREAM OF YOU by Jennifer L. Armentrout
STRIPPED DOWN by Lorelei James
RAGE/KILLIAN by Alexandra Ivy/Laura Wright
DRAGON KING by Donna Grant
PURE WICKED by Shayla Black
HARD AS STEEL by Laura Kaye
STROKE OF MIDNIGHT by Lara Adrian
ALL HALLOWS EVE by Heather Graham
KISS THE FLAME by Christopher Rice
DARING HER LOVE by Melissa Foster
TEASED by Rebecca Zanetti
THE PROMISE OF SURRENDER by Liliana Hart

On behalf of 1001 Dark Nights,

Liz Berry and M.J. Rose would like to thank ~

Steve Berry
Doug Scofield
Kim Guidroz
Jillian Stein
InkSlinger PR
Dan Slater
Asha Hossain
Chris Graham
Chelle Olsen
Kasi Alexander
Jessica Johns
Dylan Stockton
Richard Blake
and Simon Lipskar

Made in the USA
Middletown, DE
21 May 2020

95601798R00073